A Fistful of Diamonds

a gemstone thriller

Gemstone Thrillers *by* John B. Robinson

The Sapphire Sea
A Fistful of Diamonds

A Fistful of Diamonds

a gemstone thriller

John B. Robinson

[signature: John B. Robi...]

McBooks Press, Inc.
www.mcbooks.com

Ithaca, NY

Published by McBooks Press, Inc. 2008
Copyright © 2008 by John B. Robinson

Dust jacket, cover and book design by Panda Musgrove.
Maps of Africa adapted from *The 2008 World Fact Book,* a publication of the U.S.
Government.
Cover images used under license of Shutterstock.com:
Copyright © 2007, Baloncici and Ovidiu Iordachi.

The hardcover edition of this title was cataloged as:

Library of Congress Cataloging-in-Publication Data

Robinson, John B., 1968–
 A fistful of diamonds : a gemstone thriller / John B. Robinson.
  p. cm.
 Summary: "[Gem-expert Lonny Cushman travels to Rwanda in search of a price-
less suite of green diamonds]"—Provided by publisher.
  ISBN 978-1-59013-150-3 (alk. paper) — ISBN 978-1-59013-163-3 (trade pbk.:
alk. paper)
 1. Americans—Rwanda—Fiction. 2. Diamond industry and trade—Fiction. 3.
Rwanda—Fiction. I. Title.
 PS3618.O327F57 2008
 813'.6—dc22
                    2008027193

All McBooks Press titles can be ordered by calling toll-free 1-888-BOOKS11
(1-888-266-5711). Please call to request a free catalog.

Visit the McBooks Press website at www.mcbooks.com.

Printed in the United States of America
9 8 7 6 5 4 3 2 1

For Thomas Kamilindi, a living light,
proof that the power of love sweeps away the darkness.

Rwanda

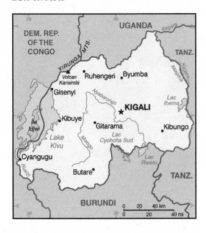

Democratic Rep. of the Congo

Republic of the Congo

A Fistful of Diamonds

a gemstone thriller

1 Back in the Game

Even among gem dealers accustomed to greasing blood-stained palms, Rwanda enjoyed a hellish reputation. In the last forty years the tiny Central African country had hosted four major genocides on top of its current blitzkrieg of the Congo. Three million were newly dead, hacked in stadiums, soccer fields, schools and churches, and though the international spotlight flickered briefly on the worst of the slaughter, daily massacres were still happening off camera. Fourteen-year-old guerillas and drug-addled veterans burned villages, kidnapped children, and committed other freelance atrocities that added corpses by the thousands every week.

Lonny Cushman focused on the positives. It was October, 2000. Wall Street was roaring. The New York Mets were crushing the San Francisco Giants in the National League play-offs. There was a matching suite of ten green diamonds waiting for the first buyer who entered the killing zone. And he was traveling under the perfect alibi. Ethnic warfare was a business, but not his business.

Last aboard the 9:35 a.m. flight from Brussels to Kigali, Lonny strolled down the concourse with the studied nonchalance of a stage performer. He had spent the previous night in Antwerp, haggling the price of a 6.018 carat, fancy intense-blue diamond with an aged Belgian diamantaire. They had been unable to agree on terms in spite of a three-course meal, bottles of vintage Bordeaux, shots of Finnish vodka, and fruitless appeals to each other's sense of *rakhmones*—compassion.

A steward led him through the plush first-class cabin seated with impeccably dressed Africans, past the roomy business section occupied by a rainbow coalition of diplomats, aid workers, and United Nations personnel, to the tourist section in the far back crammed to overflowing with a sea of white faces—volunteer math teachers, missionaries, and human-rights advocates.

They squeezed behind a slender young woman pushing a carry-on bag into the overhead compartment. In one glance at the side of her face, like any man of the world, Lonny took note of her distinctive feminine signature. Not that she was especially beautiful, or her elongated figure was particularly remarkable, but he was drawn to something naïve and vulnerable in her sharp features. He felt the need to look at her one more time. As he did, she turned her head. Her liquid blue eyes rested on his face with benign attention, as if she recognized something familiar in him too, then she looked past his shoulder to the steward.

The steward said, "Here you are, sir."

Lonny waited for his seatmate to arrange herself in the middle before he bounced the magazine against the palm of his hand and claimed the aisle. She had bobbed black hair that curled under her chin, and her eyebrows were shaped into dark swooshes against her alabaster skin. She was wearing faded blue jeans, a tight cotton sweater, and rectangular reading glasses with lapis lazuli–colored frames. She could have been a sexy college student traveling on a research grant.

"Ms. Alice Carpenter, I presume?"

"Who are you?"

"Leonard Cushman. I'm on the Board of the Cathedral of St. John the Divine." He offered his hand, which she shook with a wary, hesitant grip.

"What are you doing here?"

"Didn't your boss tell you I was coming?"

"Dean Addison?"

"He asked me to chaperone you to Rwanda." Dean Addison had touted the precocious nineteen-year-old as the future of the Episcopal Church. She had already been ordained a deacon; if she graduated from seminary the following year, she was on track to become the youngest female priest in Anglican history. She had been given a plum job at St. John's because the Bishop of New York supported the emerging field of theological feminism.

The seminarian raised her dramatic eyebrows at the gem dealer. She opened her mouth, shut it. Opened it again, closed it again. Her right hand balled into a fist around her thumb. She finally managed to get her vocal chords and emotions working at the same time. "That turkey!"

Lonny felt an intense flicker of biological attraction at her girlish indignation. The passenger in the window seat, a fat European engineer reading a technical manual, nodded cheerfully at the two Americans. Lonny wiggled his fingers in greeting. Bedding a student priest would undoubtedly punch his ticket straight to the burning canyons of hell.

"Why do you look so familiar?" she asked.

"I'm a well-known gemologist, Ms. Carpenter." He decided to keep it strictly formal.

"Oh, no, no. You can't get off that easy." She leaned toward him conspiratorially. "You're that playboy the church secretaries gossip on about. Your marital separation made Page Six of the *New York Post*." She nodded, as if she couldn't believe they were both in the same plane at the same time, sitting next to each other.

Lonny playfully bent his mouth to her ear as if making a confession. "If people call me a playboy, it's because they have no idea how I make a living."

There was more to gem dealing than zipping over to Cartier with a pair of Burmese rubies and squiring runway models. Six months before, he had been framed for the murder of a Malagasy king, been caught up in a political bloodletting, fled twenty miles into the bush, shot two soldiers, danced with the ancestors, and escaped the red island on a wooden dhow. During that entire episode he had also maintained possession of the world's most precious sapphire: 2327.39 carats in the rough, a sublime delphinium-blue color with a dazzling luminescent clarity that surpassed any stone of its kind.

She nodded, as if she totally understood. "Blood diamonds."

"No," exclaimed Lonny, momentarily taken aback. "That's not what I was saying."

"It's OK, I get it." She held a plastic water bottle to her lips and spoke into it as if she were doing a voice-over for the news hour. "The trail of tears starts here in Belgium where an international playboy boards the plane to Rwanda. Approximately six feet tall, designer-cut hair the color of baked apples, and dreamy hazelnut eyes. Why is he headed to a country where over a million citizens were murdered in 1994? What's he buying? See hair-raising footage at ten o'clock."

"Stop it." Lonny banged his knee against hers. He couldn't afford to have this conversation, and he couldn't pretend to ignore it, in case the indiscreet young scholar raised the accusation of illegal diamond trading later on. "Using an emotional term like 'blood diamonds' is a disservice to everybody in the industry."

"But it is an accurate description, isn't it?" she asked sweetly.

"No," Lonny parried. "When you give diamonds political labels, it creates inequalities. It lets the powerful monopolies that operate in 'good countries' dominate the markets. At the same time, it undervalues the work of independent miners who live in 'bad countries' because their material is not as 'pure.' The retailers just pocket the spread. There's no method short of vaporizing the diamond itself to find out if it came from the Kalahari Desert or a West African mud bank. Think about that."

"The blood diamond trade benefits the poorest Africans?"

Ms. Carpenter cross-examined him. "Is that what you're telling me?" Lonny refused the bait. There were so many colorless diamonds on earth they could pave a six-lane highway from New York to Los Angeles. And like most children raised in gem-dealing families, he'd learned to buy, split, polish, and sell the world's most fashionable stone long before he lost his virginity. The industry benchmark, a flawless, colorless, one-carat diamond, cost about the same as a used Honda Civic.

Human-rights activists coined the term "blood diamonds" to describe stones that came from the war zones of Africa. It was a catchy description and caught on like wildfire with freelance correspondents chasing the news cycle. It also totally ignored the long, brutal history of diamond mining. The Portuguese monarchy exerted its ruthless control over Brazil because of large Amazonian diamonds. The British Empire seized hold of India for the clear diamonds of Golconda and the gem treasuries of the native princes. In the greatest diamond war of them all, the Boer War of 1902, Winston Churchill and his fellow Etonians fought the Afrikaners for political control of the Kimberly mines outside Johannesburg. The most recent conflicts, in Angola, Liberia, Sierra Leone, and the Congo, were merely a continuation of the endless wrangle for money and power.

In Lonny's eyes, conflict diamonds were like twenty-dollar bills. They could build a school, vaccinate children, or buy mortars. Every woman who possessed a diamond engagement ring, a pair of *pavé* earrings, a tennis bracelet, a *bijou* around her neck, or a celebration ring on her bling finger contributed to the ever-increasing demand. He had no ethical qualms about selling the goods and neither did any diamantaire, Fifth Avenue jeweler, or mall outlet buyer he had ever met.

Naturally tinted diamonds, on the other hand, were flukes of nature so rare, so sublime and highly cherished, that only the most powerful individuals in the world ever touched one. No more than a dozen collectible-quality colored diamonds changed hands in a given year. The Tavernier, the Three Brothers, the Idol's Eye, the Bazu, the Hope, the Orlov, the Dresden Green, the Tiger's Eye, the Eureka, the Tiffany, the Brunswick Yellow, the Agra, the Hortensia, the Peach Blossom. They became national, royal, or family treasures with a name and a provenance that lasted centuries.

Lonny wasn't flying to Rwanda, stuffed into the tourist section like an empanada, because he needed money. He had divided the ninety-million-dollar windfall from the sale of the Malagasy sapphire into secure investments: sixty million placed in a binding partnership with his father, five million converted into drawers of flawless gemstones, five million stashed in mutual funds, one million for a bedroom with modern art and matching furniture, a fat offshore bank account for emergencies. As soon as his East 64th Street townhouse was renovated, he would own one of the finest addresses in Manhattan.

He was flying to Rwanda because he desperately needed to recapture the thrill of living. All around the globe, in New York, London, Antwerp, Tel Aviv, Johannesburg, Mumbai, and Bangkok, along the narrow alley of West 47th street, in Hatton Garden, the office towers of Ramat Gan, and the squalid Opera House District, gem traders battled for their lives and legacies while he viewed the action like a spectator in a box seat. The monotony of winning big was taking its toll. He was only thirty years old and he wanted to get back into the diamond game.

"Don't be upset with me," Ms. Carpenter put her hand on his arm. "I was just teasing. I don't know the first thing about gemology."

Lonny smiled graciously at her kindness. "Dean Addison told me your father was stranded in Rwanda."

"It's my job to look after my own father." Two splotches instantly appeared on her dimpled cheeks.

"The dean thought you'd need help with the African bureaucracy."

"Have you ever been to Rwanda?" She looked out the rain-streaked window, then down at the travel guide with a mountain gorilla on the cover: *Rwanda: Land of a Thousand Hills.*

"No," admitted Lonny. "But I've never been to Disney World and I still have a pretty good idea of what to expect."

Their exchange was cut short as the lights dimmed, the air crew did their rehearsed pantomime, and the plane backed away from the gate. Lonny didn't speak to his attractive charge for the next hour. He paged through a fashion magazine filled with starlets in low-cut gowns. She couldn't help seeing, sniffling with disgust whenever he lingered on a particularly revealing shot. Her idealism and sauce might have been a devastating combination over the course of a three-day love affair in Paris, but they were off to the perpetual genocide of Central Africa not the cafés of St. Germain des Prés. The plane was high above Corsica, headed toward the coast of Libya and the trackless deserts of the Sudan, when she playfully teased him again.

"Friends of mine say that all fashion is simply a degrading objectification of women."

"I'm not sure I believe that." Lonny pointed to the picture of a model in an improbable *haute couture* concoction. "I dated this chick once. She truly enjoyed being the center of attention."

Ms. Carpenter elbowed his forearm off the armrest in retaliation. "OK, I'll admit it. You're an interesting choice for a chaperone."

Lonny shoved the magazine into the seat pocket. "The dean needed me more than I needed him, I can assure you."

After his narrow escape from Madagascar six months before, he'd donated a substantial sum to the Episcopal Cathedral of St. John the Divine in memory of his mother. The titanic, tomb-like monstrosity on West 112th off Amsterdam had always been her favorite place to celebrate Christmas and Easter. An enthusiastic celebrant filled the air with billowing clouds of incense. Spotlights focused on the priests, the choir, or a gleaming gold cross. The congregation was so big that garbage cans were passed down the rows to collect donations.

The vast, dirty cathedral had been under construction for over a century and it wasn't close to completion. The wings of the central nave had never been constructed. Scaffolding surrounding the southern tower, a project from the 1980s, was fused into place. There was no money to take it down. The building's messy plight had swallowed lives, reputations, and fortunes without a burp. Perhaps that's why Lonny's suicidal mother had been drawn to it.

The ink on his check wasn't even dry before the dean of the cathedral nominated the gem dealer to the board of trustees. It was an unwelcome lesson in church politics. Lonny ignored the various committees—Justice for All Haitians, Peace in Palestine, End Hunger Now—that tried to enlist his help. He brushed off pleas from evangelicals to Save the Manatees or march in solidarity with the homeless. Then Dean Addison begged him to accompany some crazy deacon to Rwanda.

"Where are you staying in Kigali?" Lonny pushed back the top half of the seat and stretched his arms.

"I am supposed to be staying with members of the church." She emphasized the "I." "Unless you have a better idea."

"We'll find out what's going on when we get there. Why don't you tell me something about yourself? It's an eight-hour flight." He clasped his hands behind his neck.

"I confess," she said with surprising grit. "It seems like you're here to spy on me, and even though you might be an expert in these kinds of Third World situations, I find myself resenting your company."

"I made a pledge to Dean Addison to help the cathedral." Lonny stuck to his cover story. "As a priest-in-training you should be able to understand what it means to take a vow."

Ms. Carpenter sucked on her upper lip. "What does a pledge to my boss have to do with a vow?"

"The dean is the head of the cathedral. He represents the church."

"How do you know he speaks for the Lord?"

"I'm flying on faith."

"That's cute."

"Easy now," replied Lonny. "We were making small talk."

"Then tell me something about you. Something you really believe in," challenged the seminarian. She shifted in the seat and questioned him with sultry, half-closed bedroom eyes that made his heart turn over.

"Well . . ." stumbled Lonny, searching for a topic of common interest. "Like . . . the Bible." He knew the basic outline: Adam and Eve, maybe Lilith, Cain and Abel, Noah, Isaac, Moses, Mother Mary, John the Baptist, Jesus, and the apostles. He had never attended church on a regular basis. Yet even as he offered her the conversation he realized he had stepped into theological quicksand.

"Do you realize the New Testament's passages were selected and censored by a council of men three hundred years after the death of Jesus? Those men suppressed the texts that did not support their authority and elevated the ones that did. Why does everyone speak of the harsh strictures of St. Paul and not the inclusive love preached by St. Thomas? St. Thomas was edited out of the Bible! Why were the stories of only four writers chosen? Why just males?"

"I don't know." Leonard Cushman was now completely out of his depth. The foundation story of the worldwide Anglican Communion, once known as the Church of England and referred to in the United States as the Protestant Episcopal Church, was truly bizarre. It started with King Henry VIII's (1491–1547) fixation on his older brother's widow, followed by his break with Rome over the subsequent marriage and divorce. It continued with the founder's weird sexual peccadilloes, five more marriages, as well as perverse crusades against buggery and witchcraft. Lonny entertained a healthy skepticism of the motives behind the mad king's brand of religion, but he had never questioned the legitimacy of the four Gospels.

"Why do we pray to 'Our Father' who art in heaven? Why not 'Our Mother'? Or 'Our Creator'? Why do the prayer ceremonies refer to God as a Father figure? I'll tell you, because the liturgies were written by middle-aged men to support the patriarchal system they created. It's the same reason the Catholic Church let fifteen hundred years lapse before they admitted that Mary the prostitute, who came to Jesus seeking absolution, was different from Mary Magdalene, who was Jesus' female companion."

"What are you saying?" asked Lonny.

"You've swallowed the patriarchal construct hook, line, and sinker. It's the reason you've agreed to be a male chaperone. You think you can protect me. It makes you feel powerful."

Lonny rubbed his bleary eyes. "Theology aside, Ms. Carpenter, allow me to interpret my mission for you in plain English. Rwanda is a very, very dangerous place. My job is to make sure you get back to New York City alive. I couldn't give a shit about patriarchal constructs."

"You don't have to swear."

"Sorry." Lonny patted her hand.

She jerked it away as if she had been burned.

In the gem trade it was always better not to delve into the particulars of faith. Jews sold to goys, Muslims bargained with Hindus, Catholics extended credit to the Hasidim, the devout broke bread with the infidel. His father was technically Jewish, because he had a Jewish mother, but Lonny was not officially Jewish, because his own mother was a French Huguenot. The religion of Moses is tribal and can be passed down only through the maternal bloodline. The result of Lonny's muddled heritage left him a free agent. He treated Ms. Carpenter's interpretation of the New Testament with the same arm's-length skepticism he reserved for sweeping pronouncements by Talmudic scholars and the past lives of Buddhist monks.

When she buried her nose in the guidebook, probably as useful in Rwanda as a bicycle was to a fish, he rose out of his seat and brushed past the polyester curtain into business class. He needed real-time information about the current state of affairs in Kigali.

"Excuse me." Lonny interrupted an olive-skinned businessman working a laptop.

The pear-shaped merchant soaked up the New Yorker's custom-made suit, silk tie, French cuffs, and polished Italian leather shoes like a car salesman eyeing a walk-in.

"Do you speak English?" asked Lonny.

"Of course." The businessman smiled encouragingly.

"Great," continued Lonny with false cheer. "I'm an American. I'd like to—"

The man pressed his finger to his lips for silence. He heaved himself out of the wide seat and signaled Lonny to follow him to the business-class lavatories.

"My name is Suleiman." He glanced significantly toward the front of the plane, as if the Rwandan aristocrats might hear him.

"Pleased to meet you."

"How can I help?"

"I'm a missionary—"

Suleiman cut him off again with his palm. "We are men of the world, no?" His eyes traveled significantly over Lonny's expensive wardrobe. "I can't help if you are going to start with such bad lies."

"I'm an art dealer." Lonny created another tale on the spot. He had studied painting, sculpture, and textiles, and could talk about them for hours with anyone. It wasn't the first time he had used his hobby as a cover.

"What kind of art interests you?"

"Native depictions of genocide. Statues, tableaus, batiks."

Suleiman nodded in silent assent. "I'm sure you will find what you are looking for. Give me one hundred dollars."

Lonny reached into his pocket and held up a bill, honoring the first rule of gem dealing—pay to learn. Suleiman exchanged the bill for a wad of colorful Rwandan Francs. "I specialize in currency transactions."

"Very good." It was Lonny's turn to hold up the palm of his hand. "What is the safest place to stay in Kigali?"

"The Equatorial Hotel."

"Is there someone who can help me get things done?"

"The concierge at the Equatorial is the best fixer. His name is Gogo. He could find you a live gorilla if it was in his interest."

"Excellent," said Lonny. He drew out another hundred-dollar bill.

"One thing I might tell you." Suleiman plucked the second hundred dollars from Lonny's fingers as if it were a dirty tissue.

"Yes."

"Gogo works for the hotel, for himself, and others."

"Who are the others?"

Suleiman pretended he didn't hear. Lonny reluctantly fished out yet another hundred-dollar bill and stuffed it into the businessman's pocket.

"There is only one 'other' in Rwanda," said Suleiman, glancing around nervously. "The Rwandan Patriotic Army."

"Thanks for the tip," said Lonny, as the familiar, sweet dread of Mother Africa rose like bile in his throat.

"May Allah protect you."

"And you."

Lonny wandered back to his assigned seat after a decent interval. He possessed a Bachelor's degree from New York University and a Master's of Fine Arts from Columbia. He skimmed the *New York Post*, the *Daily News*, the *New York Times*, the *Wall Street Journal*, the *Financial Times*, and *Le Monde* on a daily basis. He had read plenty about Rwanda, yet the root causes behind the constant ethnic cleansings eluded him. Journalists parachuting into foreign countries rarely filed stories that dealt with much beyond the immediate misery of the situation.

His father thought Africa was for losers. Apprenticed to a distant relative during the massive pre-war exodus of 1938, Cal Cushman sailed from Odessa with a maiden aunt, was processed on Ellis Island, doused with DDT, and put to work the same day he arrived in America. His early training as a lapidary marked him with a deep suspicion of human nature. It is one thing to say a particular stone will polish out in a certain way, quite another to cut into the raw carbon and live on the result for the rest of the week.

Cal was so severely grounded to reality that imagination in any of its forms, books, music, film, held no interest. He insisted on dealing with things he could see and touch, with people he knew and trusted. His gift to Lonny was a mundane awareness of the physical. He opined that money was the one true universal language, and he never hesitated to write down a figure to make his point.

Lonny's mother bequeathed him something else entirely. A vague French belief in the possibility of transcendence. The idea that through the arts, beauty and her cousins, it was possible to elevate one's existence above banal routines. He inherited his irrational, illogical, romantic impulses from her. Without his mother's wild emotional legacy, he would have never come to love the difficult allure of black Africa.

When Lonny worried about dying in Africa, which he didn't very often because he relentlessly downplayed the negatives, his thoughts centered on Annie. She was seven years old, almost eight, learning to read and write. With Annie everything was new again. The stinky men who slept on sidewalk grates, the Empire State Building, Battery Park, high tea at the Plaza. Every explanation, every adventure was a reinterpretation of the old.

Lonny refused to allow her to call him by his first name. "You only get one father," said Lonny. "And I'm it." He wasn't going to be some New Age parent who hung out with his child's friends and did drugs with them when they became teenagers. But he didn't want to be like his father either, a distant tyrant who played by arbitrary, constantly changing rules. He wanted to be a father in all the best ways possible. Take her to the zoo, accompany the class on field trips, save her grief whenever possible.

Even though his love for Annie was so real he sometimes held on to it like a magic rope, he felt that if he was not willing to capitalize on the unprecedented opportunity to visit Rwanda under pretext of a religious mission, he might as well quit the gem trade altogether. He told her "I'll be home for your birthday" the following week.

He had won temporary joint-custody of Annie in spite of wild accusations by his soon-to-be-ex-wife, Cass, and the dire threats of her unscrupulous lawyer. The divorce, including the cost of the honeymoon and the appraised value of the engagement ring, was scheduled to go before a family-court judge in November. The final custody arrangement would be decided by a law guardian. When the scales tipped one way or the other, Lonny hoped the law guardian wasn't as hostile to the diamond industry as Ms. Carpenter pretended to be.

Lonny owed his livelihood to the forty-nine countries in sub-Saharan Africa. Nigeria and Cameroon had emeralds or pink tourmaline for sale. He bought and sold alexandrite, apatite, aquamarine, citrine, red garnets, tsavorite, tanzanite, and rubies from Kenya and Tanzania. He traded blue tourmaline, topaz, rose quartz, and diamonds from Namibia. Occasionally one heard of a spectacular diamond crystal coming out of the Congo, but there wasn't anything in Rwanda. Except green diamonds.

The flight stayed above the wispy clouds of Sudan, avoiding Uganda, currently at war with Rwanda, and flew almost to Nairobi, Kenya, before cutting east and making a beeline for Kigali. Lonny spotted the peaks of Mount Kenya sticking through the clouds like a familiar cairn. He woke the dozing scholar as they descended toward the scalped hills of central Africa. "Are you ready?"

"I'm not sure."

"Don't worry," said Lonny. "I'm going to stick to you like glue until we find out what's going on with your dad."

Ms. Carpenter scowled. "I don't want to waste your time."

"Time is like a river," Lonny replied. "You can only waste it if you think it can be possessed."

"So you're actually a Buddhist?" she asked playfully.

"I'm someone you can count on when things don't work out they way you thought they would."

Tension inside the plane increased palpably when the jet landed at Kigali International Airport. Lonny listened to the jubilant Africans, returning to their family and friends, and jostled with the morose Europeans, who had no idea of the trials ahead. Adrenaline coursed through his veins like an opiate. Once he stepped out the door, the curtain would be drawn back and the show would begin.

2 Welcome to Kigali, Mr. Cushman

The black soldiers listlessly guarding the terminal wore scuffed rubber boots and carried bruised AK-47s. The African conception of time, which is fluid and situational, usually gives no preference to the order of arrival. Lonny wasn't sure if he was more astonished at the single-file line snaking out of the terminal or the suddenly obedient masks on the faces of the powerful Rwandan elite. A lone immigration officer, slumped at a distant wooden pulpit, smudged a rubber stamp into each passport, one by one by one, as he spoke into a cell phone. The air was sticky and sweet as a trickle of sweat began an unnerving journey down the knobs of the gem dealer's spine.

Border crossings were a calculated gamble on the best of days. In Kenya, the health authorities once brandished a bent, rusty needle and threatened him with immediate immunization because his yellow fever shots were out of date. On two separate occasions, the Nigerians charged him with passport fraud and jailed him until their "suspicions" could be placated with bricks of local currency. Angolans were famous for unlubricated cavity searches.

Lonny relieved Ms. Carpenter of her passport and handed it to the officer on top of his own. The bureaucrat barely glanced at the photos while he flipped around for an empty page to smear his stamp. Smirking into the phone, he said, "Welcome to Kigali, Mr. Cushman." Lonny pulled the documents from his grip. The man held out his ink-stained fingers for the next papers in line.

The day died quickly, as always in the tropics, and in the slap of a bug it was full dark. Taxi drivers lined up in neat rows outside the terminal doors. Policemen made sure no idlers sauntered in. The luggage had already been unloaded from a baggage carousel and organized by color. Orderliness was the hallmark of every fascist regime Lonny had ever visited, as if the men in charge could expiate their crimes by keeping the sidewalks clean, and it took less than a minute to spot the telltale bank of cameras.

An orange minibus parked by the taxi stand caught Lonny's attention: the Equatorial Hotel. He drew a clump of Rwandan francs from his pocket and knocked on the passenger window. Since the authorities would want to know what a gem dealer was doing in Kigali, he decided to pitch his cover story directly to one of their informants.

"Where can I find a man named Gogo?" he asked.

The driver nodded toward the passenger, but there was no response.

"*Je cherche un homme qui s'appelle Gogo,*" he tried again in his maternal tongue.

"*Je suis Gogo,*" said the plump, acne-scarred man riding shotgun.

"A friend told me to give this to you," Lonny continued in French. He flashed the bills and slipped them into Gogo's shirt pocket.

Gogo blinked rapidly at Lonny. He was short with a small paunch. He possessed no particularly strong features, yet Lonny felt the force of the man. Gogo jerked open the van door and bounced onto the sidewalk with an outstretched hand.

"What can I do for you?"

"I'm looking for an American named Thomas Carpenter. "

"Why?"

"I'm with his daughter, Ms. Carpenter. She is very worried about his health."

"I'll see who I can talk to," replied Gogo. He examined Lonny's business card the way a pimp sums up a john, sniffing for trouble, searching for the advantage—wary, vaguely menacing, and servile. He rubbed the top of his bald pate and Lonny knew it was a signal.

As he turned to catch sight of the secret policeman, Lonny glimpsed a priest dressed in starched black robe through the plate glass windows of the terminal. He dropped Gogo and moved fast to introduce himself.

"Leonard Cushman, the Cathedral of St. John the Divine." He pumped the unsuspecting priest's hand vigorously. "Let me introduce you to Deacon Carpenter."

There was an immature pout on Ms. Carpenter's lips, which she swallowed with difficulty. "Pleased to meet you." She extended her hand honorably, but the Rwandan priest pointedly declined to make physical contact.

Instead, the priest reacted with open relief at Lonny's presence. "It is a blessing to meet you, Mr. Cushman," he said. "I am Father Rwagatera."

"Where do you have us staying for the night?" asked Lonny.

"My most heartfelt apologies," returned the soft-spoken priest. "My instructions were only to collect this . . . child from the airport."

"The dean of the cathedral asked me to chaperone Ms. Carpenter at the last minute. It is my duty to stay by her side at all times."

"Don't overdo it, Mr. Cushman," said Ms. Carpenter.

The priest glanced at her in astonishment. A Rwandan woman would never admonish a man, much less a governing member of the church, in public. "I'll take you both to the bishop's residence. His Excellency will receive you tomorrow morning."

"Very good." Lonny winked at the deacon. "It will be an honor to be a guest of His Excellency."

Lonny crammed his garment bag into the grease-stained trunk of a battered taxi and hauled the student's huge suitcase onto the roof rack, where it sat like a lotto ticket. In Lagos, Lusaka, or Johannesburg, it wouldn't have survived the trip out of the parking lot, but she didn't know that.

The wide streets were empty, the street lights dim and unevenly spaced. The Rwandan priest chatted with the driver in Kinyarwandan. The grammatically difficult language was spoken only in Rwanda, and the conversation warned Lonny that he would be dealing with an insular, tribal people. An occasional shop counter, selling warm bottles of beer, blazed with an electric light.

The taxi turned, climbed, and descended among the various hills that made up the capital of the most densely populated country in Africa. The houses were built of concrete, three or four stories tall. Although kerosene lamps glowed yellow between the jagged seams of corrugated metal shanties attached to the grander structures, the city had a cosmopolitan air. Hopelessly sprawling and sophisticated. There were no billowing heaps of plastic bags or rotting piles of garbage. There were no physical signs of the last major genocide or the ongoing war in the Congo. The wide streets had curbs, the roundabouts were well marked, metal curtains were bolted tight over shop windows.

The Bishop of Rwanda's official residence resembled a besieged outpost of the Church of England amid the Molotov cocktail–throwing Catholics of Belfast. The three-story Victorian, with a peaked roof and tall window casements, was surrounded by an ugly concrete wall, topped with concertina wire and shut off from the street by a massive metal gate. It was set apart from its neighbors by its soaring shape. The nearby houses were squat concrete structures invisible from the road.

By his inaction, Father Rwagatera forced the New Yorker to settle with the taxi driver. Priests, like celebrities and politicians, seemed to think mundane obligations like cab fare were best left to lesser, unordained mortals.

The Rwandan eventually ushered his two guests through the dirt yard, past a thick wooden door, into a drab front hall, and down a narrow corridor to closet-like rooms on the ground floor. Lonny noted the locking bolts on the outside of their doors. They were not offered a welcome of any sort. Father Rwagatera bade them a hasty good evening before retiring to a different wing of the Anglican fortress.

Lonny's narrow bed was hard, the sheets heavy and stiff. The mahogany headboard was carved with a gruesome depiction of an African Jesus carrying his cross up a Rwandan version of Calvary Hill. The bare brick walls were stained by decades of neglect. All night long Lonny lay naked atop the sheets, slapping homing mosquitoes. He could hear the seminarian doing the same in the adjoining cell, and he wondered if she was having fun yet.

He hadn't slept an entire night through in months. He usually read historical biographies or watched cable TV until he drifted off in a haze around 4 a.m. He managed to crawl out of bed by 10 a.m. and walk to work by noon, where his father goaded him mercilessly with comments like "The early bird gets the worm" or "I see Prince Charming had a busy night."

He wondered if the good deacon was pondering the unjust censorship of St. Thomas or thinking more earthy thoughts. His mind tended to wander toward the various outcomes of his divorce. Losing custody of Annie, winning custody of Annie, sharing custody indefinitely. Who would take her for vacations? How about long weekends? After-school pick up? Alimony? Child support? Divorce is a failure that calls into question other previous failures, like an Escher diagram where staircases lead back to themselves in an endless loop.

The bold rays of dawn came none too early. Lonny wiped himself down with a washcloth in the hallway sink. He squeezed into a fresh baby-blue shirt, a brilliant green Hermès silk tie, and dark conservative pinstripes he had carried for just the occasion. Ms. Carpenter knocked on the door.

"I'm hungry," she complained.

Lonny had not met the house staff the previous night, and they gave him a decidedly chilly response when he blundered into the kitchen. They had no instructions regarding the guests' breakfast. He and Ms. Carpenter were firmly directed to wait inside the bishop's office until His Excellency could receive them.

The office walls were plastered a stark Manhattan white to set off the hundreds of crucifixes attached to the bare surface. Lonny noticed the colorful plastic kind sold to bus drivers in Mexico, sleek faceless depictions fashioned from blond Swedish wood, classic Anglican models showing The Lord Our Savior with a flowing mane, a mournful face, and the title INRI—King of the Jews. Dominating the morbid collection was a four-foot-tall black Jesus with wooly hair and an ivory crown of thorns, nailed to a cross inlaid with mother-of-pearl.

Ms. Carpenter wore pressed blue jeans and a conservative cotton twin set. In spite of her best efforts to appear both older and more mature, she looked awkward, as if she were applying for her first job. When she asked quite primly for a cup of hot tea, the servants offered her a murky glass of tap water, which Lonny confiscated and poured out the window.

The bishop finally swooped in with a rustle of starched cotton. He was much smaller than the Americans, not only in height but in proportion. His hands were small, his feet were small, his head was small. He was as well formed as a black china doll. A speck of egg and a crumb of toast hung from the corner of his perfectly elliptical mouth.

"What possessed you?" were his first words.

"Excuse me?" Lonny rose from the hard chair where he had been sitting uncomfortably like a junior high truant waiting for the assistant principal.

"I specifically forbade Dean Addison from sending this notorious troublemaker to Rwanda, yet here she is."

"I am a fully invested deacon, and next year I will be a priest," Ms. Carpenter countered the accusation with steely determination.

"If we look to the scriptures," thundered the bishop, "we find that the ordination of women is an abomination before God. The Bible forbids menstrual blood to stain the holy altar. That is the reason Jesus chose men as his apostles, not women. We Africans are sick of your American lies."

Ms. Carpenter demurred, "Of all his disciples, the one Jesus loved most was Mary Magdalene."

The reply incensed the bishop, whose quavering voice rose with each word. "The New York cathedral must re-examine its commitment to the fundamental values of Christianity. Your permissive culture sanctions unwedded co-habitation, starter marriages, and homosexuality. In this country, six years after people had their faith shaken to the core by war and murder, we serve the body and blood of Our Lord Jesus Christ to the majority of the population each Sunday. The American church has lost its way in the midst of plenty. Ours has gathered strength in a time of need. The ordination of females and homosexuals is unholy and it will not abide."

Ms. Carpenter smiled politely while she skewed the man's logic. "Your defense of antiquated Roman theology is quite out of date. There is no proof that God is heterosexual. There is no proof that God is male. Women make up more than fifty percent of the human family, and we expect the same treatment from the church as we do from God."

"Now that you've both laid out your theological positions," Lonny intervened delicately, thankful his charge had maintained her composure in the face of their host's attack, "maybe we could get down to business. Bishop, the Cathedral of St. John the Divine sends your diocese one hundred thousand dollars a year. Perhaps you could show some Christian goodwill by helping Ms. Carpenter locate her father. He seems to be missing. It would mean a lot to Dean Addison."

"I have a busy day ahead of me." The bishop refused to engage him, pushing a buzzer mounted on the wall instead. The door swung open and a pair of guards in blue overalls entered the room.

"What's going on?" demanded Lonny. If this were a gem deal, he would have been halfway out the window. He backed against the desk and palmed a bronze paperweight.

In a voice dripping with condescension and contempt, the bishop addressed Ms. Carpenter. "If you so much as attend a mass in my country, I'll have you arrested."

"You can't do that," she protested.

"Try me," he mouthed from behind his desk.

The two bodyguards moved toward Ms. Carpenter. Lonny held out his hand. Enough was enough. They hadn't flown six thousand miles to be thrown out on the street like common criminals.

"Don't," he instructed.

The guard on his right threw an elbow at his head. Lonny deflected the blow with his shoulder and returned a nasty punch to the throat. The second man stepped forward to grapple, and Lonny slammed him in the heart with the paperweight.

The unarmed guards didn't know much about dirty tricks, which is all that Lonny had ever learned. He practiced once a week with a retired NYPD detective who taught him how to fight in an elevator, kick a man down a staircase, aim for the soft spots, and deliver blunt, crippling blows. Self-defense, West 47th Street style.

Lonny carefully flexed his manicured hands. "Ms. Carpenter came to you asking for help, Your Excellency. She's done nothing wrong."

Both guards groaned.

"Out," commanded the Napoleonic clergyman, impatiently pushing the buzzer.

Lonny bowed respectfully. "As a board member of St. John's, Your Excellency, I must tell you that the cathedral's financial contribution to your diocese will be under review."

Another four men escorted the visitors directly from the bishop's study to the street. They tussled again at the exterior door. One of the guards got in a slap. Lonny jabbed. A short club came down on his head and he found himself sitting in the red dust next to the deacon.

A mob of thirty or forty children encircled them both. The children had distended stomachs, eye sores, limps, oozing ear infections, mucus smeared across their faces. They threw clods of dirt and jagged pieces of gravel at Ms. Carpenter's head. Nobody came from the adjoining buildings to stop them. A twelve-year-old boy taunted the deacon with a sharpened hoe.

The mob dispersed like a flock of sparrows at the sight of Lonny staggering to his feet. Blood ran down Ms. Carpenter's forehead. Feeding off instinct, the gem dealer stepped decisively in front of a passing vehicle. He opened the rear door of the sedan and launched the religious student into the backseat. He threw a wad of Rwandan francs onto the dashboard and demanded the frightened driver take them to the Equatorial Hotel. Ms. Carpenter watched in a daze as they passed the pockmarked, battle-scarred buildings and zigzagged across the capital, up and down the hills of the indifferent city.

"You'll be OK," Lonny told her as she melted against him in the backseat, her face streaked with tears, her body wracked by sobs. "It was just a scuffle."

"I feel . . ." Ms. Carpenter panted so fast she was in danger of hyperventilating. "I feel so humiliated. I feel so wronged. He had no right to say those things. No right."

Lonny held the seminarian in his arms as she sucked the oxygen out of the fetid clunker. He felt supremely uncomfortable trying to soothe her ragged gasps. He remembered that they had left their suitcases behind at His Excellency's residence, but there was no going back. They were on their own.

. . .

Crash barriers and armed security personnel guarded the entrance to the Equatorial Hotel. There was an unmistakable poster tacked to the cinder block guardhouse displaying the types of weapons banned from that point forward: AK-47s, grenades, RPGs, pistols, machetes, and daggers. Each was depicted in silhouette, then surrounded by a red circle with a line drawn through it. The parking lot was filled to bursting with white Japanese SUVs. They were outfitted with dust snorkels, knobby tires, and air conditioning. Several had bumper stickers with land mines circled and crossed out. As if that would save them.

The hotel was a five-story monument to the nineteen sixties, fashioned from poured concrete, sliding glass doors, and miniature balconies. It could have been a Howard Johnson's with the addition of an orange roof. The reception desk was chest high, faced with cheap eucalyptus wood, and lit with recessed lighting. The lobby was bare and empty. Three clerks behind the counter helped Lonny check into two "five-star luxury suites" in the flash of a credit card. The exercise cost him six hundred dollars a night for each room. Ms. Carpenter managed to calm herself long enough to fill out the guest registration papers with a shaky hand. She refused Lonny's offer to find a doctor.

"Luggage?" asked a gaunt bellboy with salt-and-pepper hair.

"Not anymore," Lonny replied to the man's bewilderment.

The suites bore more than a passing resemblance to an American road motel: a pair of twin-size beds, a shower-bath, a TV, and a balcony overlooking what had to be the only swimming pool in Central Africa. Ms. Carpenter locked herself in her room as soon as she reached it. Lonny called the front desk for a fan to compensate for the egregious lack of air conditioning, then stretched out and fell asleep before it was delivered.

The oppressive stench of late morning crept through the open window within the hour. Lonny, still wearing his pinstripes and tie as if it were a protective suit of armor, went back down to the lobby, swiped a tourist map from the front desk, and wandered out the door of the hotel. He wanted to get a feel for Kigali before it swallowed him alive.

One side of the map was a straightforward tourist guide with restaurants, hotels, and travel agencies marked with numbers; the numbers corresponded to a legend. Advertisements ringed the edge with logos, telephone numbers, and postal addresses. The flip side of the map displayed stomach-turning photos of the 1994 genocide in living color and marked the locations where the atrocities took place. One photo showed a pile of dead children stacked like puppets. Another graphically focused on the scorched body of a woman with her legs spread open. Yet another depicted a group of men who had their necks wired so tightly together they strangled each other. Each photo was accompanied by a detailed explanation in English that left no room for positive interpretation. It made the grainy black-and-white pictures of Nazi atrocities seem quaint by comparison.

Lonny meandered up the hill through a district of four-story office buildings and retail shops. On the ground floor of what had been RTLM, Hutu Power Radio, he bought a bitter cup of coffee. Six years before, the radio station had broadcast execution lists and calls to murder 24 hours a day for 100 days. More than 300,000 moderate Hutus and Tutsis were hacked, lynched, burned, starved, bludgeoned, raped to death, suffocated, run over, and drowned in Kigali as the extremists seized power. Lonny continued in a grand circle past a hospital, which the map told him had been packed with 25,000 casualties at the height of the terror and onward to a neighborhood of expensive houses where a blotch of paint marked the spot where the Tutsi prime minister was assassinated. She and the other moderate politicians were methodically eliminated in the beginning of the slaughter.

He continued walking until he reached a roundabout at the end of a street. The map told him he was standing next to the remains of

the old presidential palace. Cross streets were blockaded with concrete barriers and sandbagged machine gun positions. He tried to
approach the American Embassy, a sturdy building surrounded by a
blast wall and flying the American flag, but grim Rwandan soldiers
waved him away without explanation. He walked past the military
barracks at the other end of the street where ten UN Peacekeepers
had been kidnapped, beaten, tortured, and executed. Reeling from
the debacle in Somalia that had killed sixteen U.S. Army Rangers,
the international community abandoned Rwanda to its dark fate
immediately afterward.

It was with some relief that Lonny stumbled back upon the intersection near the hotel. A hoard of maimed women and brutally
deformed children rushed him before he could get to the guardhouse. Several of the women were missing limbs, one girl had a dent
the size of a baseball in her forehead. Their awful sores provoked
more revulsion than pity. He shouted, *"Acha,"* go away, in Swahili, to
no effect. He tossed a sheaf of bills in the air. The mutilated women
tore into one another, and he bolted. It reminded him of the day he
foolishly toured Mumbai without a guide. A gang of professional
beggars had pursued him so diligently and so aggressively that he
finally turned his pockets inside out and offered up his shoes.

Inside the protection of the hotel walls, he made a desultory pass
through the gift shop. A shelf of books related to the six-year-old
genocide and war: *At the Bottom of the Pile: Eyewitness Accounts of the
World's Most Horrific Massacres; The Day They Came for My Babies;
Death, Despair, and Defiance.* He purchased Dian Fossey's autobi-
ography, *Gorillas in the Mist,* and a World Bank report, *Rwanda: A
Case Study in Catastrophic System Failure.*

He descended to the restaurant on the ground level and picked
a well-shaded table next to the heavily chlorinated pool. It was
about 11:30 a.m. Swarms of waiters, bellhops, cleaners, workmen,
and clerks moved briskly throughout the hundred-room hotel.
According to his trusty map, the hotel itself had sheltered two

thousand people for the duration of the genocide. Guests drank water from the pool and bartered sex for dry biscuits.

Discussion groups of expatriates now clustered around poolside tables, consulting laptop computers, munching croissants, and sipping fresh-squeezed orange juice. A representative from Condom Sense International had a briefcase of purple condoms displayed. Lonny was well aware that every "aid worker" received a five-digit monthly salary, rented a house with three or more servants, and drove one of the sixty-thousand-dollar SUVs parked in the lot. They reminded Lonny of the carpetbaggers who swept in behind Sherman and devoured the old Confederacy after the ravages of war reduced the original inhabitants to starvation.

"What can I do for you, sir?" greeted an impeccably turned-out waiter. He sported a white shirt, black vest, tailored pants, and a red apron.

"You serve breakfast at this hour?" asked Lonny.

"We have a full menu, sir."

"I'd like a cheese and pepper omelet," said Lonny. "Fried potatoes, ketchup, and a bottle of mineral water."

"Perrier or San Pellegrino?"

"Perrier."

"Excellent choice, sir."

Within the space of a few minutes, Lonny had traversed the moat separating uninterrupted despair from unnecessary luxury. There was never a middle ground in Africa. The World Bank report confirmed his suspicions that Rwanda was going to be sucking the international tit for decades to come. Dian Fossey's book started off with the generous self-delusions of an occupational therapist determined to change her life by visiting Africa, and ended with a postscript about her murder in the Virunga Mountains. It didn't take long to surrender the futility of optimism and order the first vodka tonic of the day.

· · ·

An enormous African with a rich West African baritone put a hand on Lonny's shoulder, "You must be Leonard." He was over six feet tall and weighed three hundred and fifty plus pounds. His skin was the deep, velvety black of a clan who do not marry the light-skinned cousins. He wore a cotton print shirt, khakis, and polished leather shoes. "My name is Ibrahim."

"From Senegal?" Lonny sprang to his feet and stretched out his hand. "I've been searching for you."

"Not very hard." Ibrahim raised both eyebrows at the vodka.

"I knew you would find me."

"It is the will of Allah." Ibrahim bowed his shaved head. He wore a gold chain in his ear, several more around his neck, and a pinky ring that must have weighed a Krugerrand. "Waiter, bring me a gin tonic and the backgammon board."

"I didn't think Muslims drank before noon."

"You know," said Ibrahim, "I was arrested for having a drink not too long ago."

"Tell me about it."

"Ehh!" bellowed Ibrahim. "I tried to enter Israel through Tel Aviv. The Jewish border guards laughed and laughed. They said, 'No Muslim with black skin and a black skull is getting into our country to blow up our boys and girls.' The Israelis put me on a plane to Dubai. There was a technical malfunction over Saudi Arabia. The plane landed in Riyadh. The Islamic border guards checked my documents, 'Why do you have an Israeli stamp in your passport?'

"I said, 'I am a citizen of Senegal. I have the right to travel to any country. If I want to go to North Korea you can't stop me!'

"They said, 'Ibrahim, you're a Muslim. Muslims can't go to Israel.'

"I told them, 'I never got into Israel. I was kicked out of Tel Aviv.'

"'Tel Aviv is Israel,' they say.

"'You're scrambled,' I tell them. 'I don't want to come to your country either.'

"I was sentenced to three days in jail. My parents are going crazy. Ehh! They thought the Jews murdered me. 'It wasn't the Israelis,' I told them. 'I was kidnapped by the mujahideen!'

"When I got to Dubai, I find a true Christian watering hole, 'Luke's Bar.' It is, my brother, an oasis in the desert. I ordered English gin and Schweppes in a tall glass with ice cubes, *comme il faut.* Ten minutes later I'm arrested again. It's illegal for a Muslim to drink alcohol during Ramadan in Dubai! I tell them, 'Are you crazy? I'm from Senegal. I'm in a Christian bar. I was expelled from Israel because I'm Muslim. I was jailed in Saudi Arabia because I was in Israel. Now you people won't let me have my gin tonic!' Three more days in jail.

"The Israelis called me yesterday. They wanted to buy me another plane ticket to Tel Aviv and I said, 'From now on you come to Africa. It's safer!'"

"*Santé,*" offered Lonny.

"*Santé,* my brother," toasted Ibrahim, clinking his glass. "I understand you want green stones."

"Yes," said Lonny.

"Your father is the best colored-diamond dealer in New York."

"My father and I are partners," confirmed Lonny. "He told you I was coming?"

"He did."

"Well?"

"I might have some business for you."

"What are the trade conditions in this country?"

Ibrahim arranged the backgammon pieces as he carefully framed a response. "There is a section of the Rwandan government called the Congo Desk. The Congo Desk is responsible for supplying the Rwandan Patriotic Army with its operating budget. To come up with that money, it oversees the disposition of goods looted from the Democratic Republic of Congo. Any Rwandan military officer found selling diamonds, coltran, or ebony originating in the DRC is considered a traitor. Foreigners caught trafficking the same goods are labeled criminals and also risk execution. I am a licensed jeweler, not a military officer. I am allowed to buy, sell, or possess diamonds in the pursuit of my profession.

"If they find a white man like you with so much as an ebony toothpick sticking out of his mouth, they're going to dig a shallow grave and bury you alive."

"Just as I hoped," Lonny grinned. It was the reason none of the other top dealers dared venture into Central Africa. Even the lure of green diamonds couldn't stiffen their spines. They preferred to wait patiently until the material gravitated toward their own webs of power and influence. That's what gave Lonny his edge—his willingness to jump into the void while others shook their heads in stunned disbelief.

Ibrahim moved his pieces aggressively across the board. Lonny countered with a sacrifice and a trap.

"Five dollars apiece?" wagered Ibrahim.

"Only if you have another drink with me."

"*Mazal*," replied Ibrahim in Yiddish, the *lingua franca* of international diamond trade, as he nailed Lonny. "That hurts."

They continued sparring while Ibrahim ordered *confit de canard, pommes au gratin,* and *haricots verts.* During their sixth game Lonny let slip, "I am also looking for a missing person."

Ibrahim set the doubling die so that they were playing for ten dollars apiece. "I cannot help you find a missing person. But I can tell you where to start looking."

"Where?"

"At the Tech Café. They sell mobile phones to everyone in this country. They may have this missing person's telephone number on file."

"That's helpful," said Lonny, turning the doubling die again so they were playing for twenty dollars apiece. By 2 p.m. Ibrahim owed Lonny two thousand dollars.

"I didn't know Americans could play backgammon."

"It seems there is a lot you don't know about Americans. Were you expecting to beat me?"

"I don't play to lose."

"Me neither."

Ibrahim took out a massive roll of one-hundred-dollar bills and laid twenty on the table. "Flip a coin, double or nothing."

"Whose coin?"

"Mine."

"Allow me to toss."

"No, I'll flip it."

"Not for my money."

They both laughed.

Their gambling was interrupted by the spectacular appearance of Ms. Carpenter. She hadn't changed her clothes or taken a shower in the past four hours. A streak of dried blood ran from her forehead to her chin. Large patches of sweat stained her underarms. She approached the table unsteadily and said to Lonny, "I think I need your help."

"My telephone number," Ibrahim passed Lonny a business card. "Buy a mobile. Call me later." They shook hands, and Ibrahim hastily excused himself as if he suspected Ms. Carpenter of spreading the Ebola virus.

"You're scaring the natives," said Lonny.

"I need your help," she repeated.

"You need some first aid." Lonny grasped her firmly by her elbow and steered her toward the front desk. The clerks sold him a clear plastic bag that contained everything to treat a gunshot wound. Scissors, sutures, gauze, hydrogen peroxide, ointment, tape. She clearly wasn't the first guest to require hospital supplies.

They went up to Ms. Carpenter's bathroom.

"Owee, owee, owee," she cried out, as Lonny poured the hydrogen peroxide into her hairline. The bloody liquid ran into the sink.

"Let me hire a doctor to take care of this."

"I don't want a Rwandan doctor to touch me!" shouted Ms. Carpenter, on the verge of tears.

"Dial it back, sister," said Lonny. "If you want to be mad at His Excellency, go ahead. But don't take it out on the whole world."

"OK," she said finally, her blue eyes staring into his. "I know you're right. But I'm mad and I'm scared."

He swabbed the wound with gauze and made up a bulky bandage. "Take a shower," he advised her. "It'll make you feel better."

"Are you going to take a shower with me?"

"What?"

"I should probably do this alone."

"I forgot." Lonny flashed a quick smile. "You're an introvert." He retreated to the hotel room. There was no movement for an instant; then, through the thin paperboard door, he could hear her climb into the shower without undressing. After a few minutes of water on cotton, he heard loud, uncontrollable sobs and thought the worst might be over.

3 Congo Green

Alice Carpenter stepped into the room wearing a short hotel bathrobe that barely covered her hips. Her raven hair was tangled in knots over the white gauze. Her delicate skin was cherry red from the scalding water she had used to scrub off an entire layer of cells. But there was still mischief in her eye when she asked, "Are you going to let me dry off?"

"I'm not moving until we get a few things straight," replied Lonny, feeling impervious to her evident charms. "You obviously knew the bishop's views before the meeting. You weren't about to change his interpretation of the Bible. So why did you argue with him?"

"He started it!"

Lonny chewed his thumbnail. Ms. Carpenter reminded him of Annie when she couldn't have something she really wanted, like a chocolate ice cream cone in the winter or a pair of pink, patent leather Mary Janes. Lonny suspected there was some deep hurt he couldn't touch, and would probably never uncover, gnawing away at her core. Maybe that's why she chose to enter a profession dominated by old men whose baseline reasoning hadn't changed in centuries. It gave her an easy target.

"What's your major problem?" he demanded. "What is it that makes you so angry?"

"Injustice makes me angry."

"Well," he tried to control his exasperation. "It's dangerous to voice the wrong opinion around here."

"I'm not going to stop fighting for my rights," she returned, spreading her arms like Moses come down from on high. "Power will eventually bow to truth."

"Are you insane?" If he had ever claimed anything as patently idealistic in his student days, his father would have delivered a biff-whack so hard his forehead would have crashed into the Statue of Liberty and snapped back into Coney Island. "We're in a country that sells tourist maps marked with massacre sites. They publicize their history of intolerance like it's a marketable attraction."

"Let's agree to put aside what happened this morning," Ms. Carpenter said bravely. "Right now, I need to find my father. That's all that matters."

Now we're getting somewhere, thought Lonny. Arrested development, patriarchal constructs, adolescent tantrums—her father. The day he figured out the relationship with his own father, he'd be a new person.

"Why did he come to Rwanda?" Lonny asked.

"I don't know, exactly."

"Then why do you need to find him?"

She spoke peevishly, as if he already knew the answer. "He borrowed $250,000 from St. John the Divine two months ago. I haven't heard from him since."

Lonny bit the inside of his cheek. "You lost me."

Ms. Carpenter leaned against the wooden headboard, allowing her long legs to stretch across the bed. "My father had a lead on something that would make millions for the cathedral. Dean Addison invested with my father and, unfortunately, that's the last we saw of him."

"So you've come to get the money back?"

"More or less."

"What happens if you can't find your father?"

"I'll get booted out of seminary."

"Because of a bad investment?"

She glared at him, as if she really didn't believe she needed to say the words out loud. "My father insisted Dean Addison lend him the money off the books. He didn't want anything traced back to the church because the investment was controversial. The Dean signed a check over to me. I gave it to my dad. Now the quarterly budget review is approaching and the money is gone. I need to account for that $250,000 quick."

"A deacon makes $21,000 a year." Lonny had paged through the annual report and could remember figures the way the Bishop of Kigali could quote Leviticus. "Why would your father put you on the line for a quarter of a million bucks?"

"I don't know," said Ms. Carpenter, the emotional roller coaster of the morning plainly showing in the deflating bags under her eyes. "My mom divorced him when I was eight. My younger sister and I never had much contact with him."

"That's the man you convinced Dean Addison to entrust with the cathedral's endowment?"

"I owed him one chance to prove himself."

"In Rwanda?"

"He mentioned diamonds."

"Your long-lost, deadbeat father is on a jag with church money?" Lonny couldn't believe his ears. Flying on a hope and a briefcase of cash, thousands of dilettantes tried to enter the diamond business each year. One or two made money by happenstance. A few more broke even out of dumb luck and returned to the suburbs of New Jersey with tales of high adventure. The other 99.99% lost everything, including spare body parts, to the pros. Starting out in Rwanda was like playing Russian roulette with a semiautomatic pistol.

"What's that supposed to mean? It's all my fault?"

"Do you have a picture?"

"Of course." Ms. Carpenter retrieved a wallet photo of a man in his mid-sixties. Graying temples, thin face, sagging cheeks. A dad like any other.

"It's not all your fault." Lonny felt an uncharacteristic rush of sympathy for the girl. They'd be lucky to locate her father's body in a mass grave. White men with large amounts of cash and little common sense had the lifespan of a gnat in Central Africa. "You think life ought to be fair. That everything should work out if you play by the rules."

"That would be nice," said the student, wrapping her arms around her head so that he couldn't see her face.

"I'll be back before nightfall." Although she had the breasts, hips, and thighs of a woman, and the education, job title, and responsibilities of an adult, it dawned on him that she was no more than a confused teenager. "For your own safety, please don't leave the room."

Lonny took a taxi across Kigali to the Tech Revolution, Central Africa's Cyber Café. In the harsh afternoon glare, the capital city seemed to stagger under the weight of its violent history. The national parliament building was shot through with so many holes it looked as if it would melt in a hard rain. The driver explained that back in April, 1994, a battalion of American-trained Tutsi troops bunkered down in the basement while the French-trained Hutu military blasted them with rockets. The Tutsi finally broke out, fought their tormentors to the death, and liberated the city. They went on to rout the presidential guard and chase the Hutu leadership into the Congo.

Patches of corn were planted behind the buildings and in the traffic circles. There were no street vendors selling food, no dogs, and no garbage. To Lonny's well-traveled eye, it added up to clear signs of famine.

The Tech Café was an immaculate, bright storefront with six

computers and a shiny sales counter. Located between a barbershop and music kiosk, it seemed as if it had been dropped out of the sky by a Kansas twister.

"I'd like to buy a phone," said Lonny.

"Who are you with?" came the reply in perfect American English. The clerk was a dude with wire-rimmed glasses. The President's picture looked down at Lonny over the man's shoulder and forced him to do a double take. The clerk had groomed himself exactly like the Head of State.

"I'm here by myself." Using Ms. Carpenter as an excuse to enter Rwanda was far too easy. He knew there was going to be a catch.

"You work for a nongovernmental agency?"

"No."

"You work for an embassy."

"No.

"You a member of a foreign military contingent."

"No."

"What are you doing here?"

"I want a phone."

"Who are you attached to?"

"I'm a tourist."

"Ah," said the clerk. "You are here to see the gorillas."

"Yes indeed." Lonny relaxed. "Dian Fossey is one of my heroes."

It took an hour to buy the phone. He was required to complete a two-page application, submit four photos (which required a taxi ride across town and back), present a photocopy of his passport, and arrange a credit reference from the hotel. Cell phones were a military priority. The government had put up towers across the country and reception was digitally clear in the major towns. It cost him several likenesses of Ben Franklin to prepay six hundred minutes of airtime and rush the paperwork.

"I also need the telephone number of a friend," said Lonny, when the phone was safely in hand.

"We don't give out telephone numbers."

"It would take a second to look it up."

"We are not allowed to give that information."

"How am I supposed to call my friend?"

"When you see your friend, ask for his number."

"I don't know where my friend is, that's why I want to call him."

"No can do," said the clerk.

It's possible to pay a person to do their assigned job, like issue a visa at a border crossing. It's also possible to pay a person not to do their job, like asking a policeman to look the other way. But it is extremely difficult to bribe a person to do something that is against the rules. No matter how much money Lonny slid across the glass countertop, he doubted he would get Thomas Carpenter's correct phone number. Even dudes balk at the insult of an outright bribe.

"May I rent one of your computers to send an e-mail?"

"No problemo," replied the President's body double.

Lonny logged on to his New York server by satellite and sent his daughter the following message:

> *Dear Annie, I am in the land of big hairy gorillas. I'll bring one home if they let me. Not sure where we'd keep him though, maybe your room. Hope school is great. Love, Daddy.*

To his father, he wrote: *I am at the Equatorial Hotel.*

Lonny included neither salutation nor signature in this last message. If the government was going to track his cell phone use, he had no doubt they could read his e-mails.

Back at the Equatorial Hotel, Lonny cornered Gogo at the shoe-shine stand next to the front door. The concierge was standing on day-old newspaper while his loafers received a fresh coat of shiny black wax. There was a camera covering the parking lot. Lonny stepped underneath its range.

"Have you found Ms. Carpenter's father?"

"Patience, please."

"It's become an urgent matter." Lonny laid a crisp hundred-dollar bill in Gogo's palm. "I need Thomas Carpenter's cell phone number right now."

"You tip like a missionary."

"Will a thousand dollars get the job done?" asked Lonny. He carried $20,000 in cash, divided into unequal stashes and jammed into six separate pockets. His method allowed him to show varying amounts to different people under different circumstances. Thieves were usually satisfied with the contents of one or two pockets, corrupt border guards with as many as three. Few would suspect that Lonny carried one thousand in his wallet, six thousand in his back left pocket, four thousand in his front left, four thousand in one inside suit pocket, three thousand in the other, another two thousand in his money belt. Hard currency was the lifeblood of his business.

He reached into his shirt pocket and flashed Gogo the sheaf of hundred-dollar bills he had taken off Ibrahim.

"For a thousand dollars," said Gogo, "I will find out who this man is sleeping with!"

Lonny left Gogo in his socks and walked into the parking lot to dial Ibrahim's number on his new toy. Even if the government could listen to every cell phone in the country, he doubted they had the capability of monitoring more than a dozen phones simultaneously. He hadn't done anything yet to attract high-level attention.

"Where are you?" he said to Ibrahim

"Take a taxi to my store," replied the Senegalese. "It's in the lower market."

"When should I come over?"

"Now."

Lonny warily approached the line of taxis parked near the guardhouse. The taxi that took him from the hotel to the Tech Café cost him two hundred Rwandan francs. Another that drove him around half of Kigali looking for a passport photo charged ten francs. The cost was insignificant, it was the principle. He didn't like being taken for a sucker.

He argued with five drivers. The negotiations followed a similar pattern: the hills were steep, the lower market was crowded, gas cost so much these days—one hundred and fifty francs. The drivers spoke English and stuck to their price.

"I'm not a bank dressed in a white skin," declared Lonny, exasperated by his inability to get the drivers to break ranks.

"We're not niggers working for pocket change," one driver countered. "When our people were being hacked, you Americans changed the channel."

"Am I supposed to pay for Belgian colonialism too?" demanded Lonny.

"You're a Big Man. You can afford three hundred and fifty francs."

"It's not about who's rich and who's poor. It's about the right price."

"For you, three hundred and fifty francs."

Lonny almost took his chances walking to the lower market before an absolute brick of a human being intervened. The stocky man was as wide as he was tall. A fireplug draped in garments. He glared at the other taxi drivers with evident distaste while touching Lonny's forearm lightly.

"Jean-Batiste," the man introduced himself.

"*Alors.*" Lonny picked up the conversation in French. Since his map exercises and the World Bank report, Lonny understood that if he were speaking French he was conversing with a genocide survivor. If he were speaking English, he was conversing with a member of the Tutsi diaspora who had grown up in Uganda, Kenya, or Tanzania, and only recently returned to rule the country after the end of the 1994 war. "How much will you charge to take me to the lower market?"

"*Dix francs.*" Ten francs.

"*On y va,*" said Lonny. Let's go.

The 1970s diesel Mercedes had those rounded fenders that Africans jokingly referred to as "Monicas," after President Clinton's voluptuous intern. The car was deep burgundy with a lopsided dent in the roof. Lonny climbed aboard. The other taxi drivers tsk-tsked with disapproval as the French-speaking driver passed them.

"You're in trouble," said Lonny.

"I'll blow them to pieces if they even sneeze my direction." The driver reached under the seat and held out a live hand grenade.

"Very nice. Do you know the jeweler Ibrahim's shop?"

"Everyone knows it."

They drove down the hill past the Church of St. Famille. According to Lonny's four-color map, thousands had been saved at the church. Several hundred had also been betrayed by a pistol-packing Catholic priest who cooperated with the *interhamwe*.

During the '94 genocide, the *interhamwe* were a group of young men and women whose name translated as "those who work to-gether." They wore baggy, hip-hop clothing and carried spiked clubs. If they caught a person without ID or carrying an ID card marked "Tutsi," they immediately bludgeoned their victim to death. Their name—so specific and so terrifying the mere mention of it caused fainting, heart attacks, and suicide—was now a generic label used to brand any enemy of the Tutsi government.

Streets near the lower market were narrow enough that the passage seemed like an open tunnel. Pedestrians forced off the pavement reached out their hands automatically at the sight of Lonny's white face. All the successful European businessmen had fled in droves during the last genocide. The smattering of whites who returned were simply in charge of giving things away. A boy selling individual sheets of Kleenex gestured feebly. His eyes were glazed with a cloudy film. An oozing, puckered scar ran across the top of his head like a fleshy Mohawk.

Ibrahim's lair was a miserable concrete box encased with iron window grills, bracketed by two identical buildings painted the same piss yellow with bare zinc doors. Only somebody who knew exactly where it was located would be able to find it.

"This is the shop?" asked Lonny

"I'll wait for you." Jean-Batiste laid the smooth Soviet grenade on his lap.

Lonny pushed an intercom switch. "*Salaam alekam.* It's me." The lock on the solid metal door hummed, and Lonny shouldered it open. It took a moment for his pupils to adjust to the unusual darkness of the jewelry store. It was somber enough that a chunk of spinel could pass for a ruby. The walls were lined with sooty crimson velour and trimmed with dark wood. A single fluorescent tube flickered from the ceiling. The display cases contained gold filigree work from cheap Indian bazaars.

"Come in the back," shouted Ibrahim.

Lonny walked gingerly around the counter. The hulking Senegalese dealer was seated at a workbench that consisted of a board propped up on crates. He was wearing his usual outfit, not a jeweler's leather apron or magnifying lamp in sight. A couple of tools lay about. There didn't seem to be a vise or a forge. The floor was pounded clay.

"What do you think of my store?"

"It smells like a shepherd's hovel," replied Lonny. The African diamantaire would have been challenged to squeeze a polished citrine into a prong setting at his teetering workbench.

"I want you to see something," said Ibrahim. He poured a film canister of rough diamonds onto a white sheet of paper. To the untrained eye they would have looked like large crystals of salt, serrated and opaque. Except for one that was off-color.

"Give me light."

Ibrahim handed him a cheap plastic flashlight with a weak incandescent bulb. Lonny rolled the abraded pebble on the palm of his hand. The radiation that gave the stone its color had burned its "skin" a millimeter or two in depth.

Lonny's pulse raced as he put it on top of the flashlight. "How much does it weigh?"

"1.637 carats."

"What do you want from me?" He felt the heat rise on his forehead with the expectation of Ibrahim's reply. The African dealer would probably offer him a cheap price for an immediate transfer to an offshore bank account. Every dealer had one.

"A partnership. The guy who sold me this stone had nine more. Five or six carats each. Incredible material."

"A matching suite?" Lonny's heart thudded uncontrollably at the prospect while he tried to overcome his disappointment in the actual stone. He had been privileged to examine several hundred fancy diamonds because of his father's long involvement in the trade. When he used his mind's eye to compare those stones to the one before him, none of them shared the same characteristics. But then the light would have been better in a 2nd Avenue strip joint.

"I need a partner who can wire five million dollars on ten-minutes' notice. Can you do it?"

"Absolutely." From Ibrahim's description, the stones would fetch twenty million dollars, and it was out of the question to take possession in Rwanda. Lonny would have to put up the money and trust Ibrahim to deliver the entire suite to New York. Then Ibrahim would have to trust Lonny to make the final sale. They were asking a lot from each other for two guys who had just met earlier in the day.

"What's the origin of the suite?"

"Why?"

"I can't auction a collectible-quality colored diamond without a verified source."

"Eh!" Ibrahim laughed. "There are no roads in the Congo. Last year I bought a canary yellow diamond the size of your dick. I wanted to finance more excavation. The diggers couldn't remember where they had been!"

"This came from the Congo?"

Ibrahim closed his mouth and wagged his finger. "Ehh, ehh, ehh, you want to be partners or not?"

"I need to think it over." If the stone were a fake, the dealer would pressure him to close the deal immediately.

"Diamonds wait for no man."

"We'll have breakfast tomorrow." Lonny nudged the dark speck.

"My store is giving you second thoughts?"

"I've seen nicer crack dens."

"You don't appreciate the way I do business," laughed Ibrahim. "If I had a clean, well-lighted place, the Rwandan Patriotic Army would cut off my genitals and stuff them down my throat."

"Hmm . . ." Lonny tried to picture the other stones in his mind.

Ibrahim told him, "Sleep on it."

The ride back to the hotel with Jean-Batiste gave Lonny critical time to think. Auctioning a suite of ten green diamonds would be a great coup. Fronting Ibrahim five million dollars might also result in his swift arrest—if Ibrahim kept the diamonds, stole the money, and had Lonny detained to cover his tracks. A routine maneuver the world over. He needed a lot more information about Ibrahim.

Lonny dialed his father's number. Cal was one of a dozen experts in the industry whose niche was colored diamonds—a specialist inside a profession of generalists. Other dealers called him when they came across something they couldn't handle. He had been in the business for fifty years and was on a first-name basis with all the families that mattered. Ibrahim's father had initially contacted Cal three months ago.

"Is that you?" demanded Cal Cushman, eight time zones away.

"It's me." Lonny completed the routine.

"How is it?"

"I've seen the green."

"What now?"

"The man here wants me to buy in."

"Green is a difficult color," cautioned his father. "It can be faked many different ways."

Here we go, thought Lonny. A matching suite of natural green diamonds was the statistical equivalent of squeezing a camel through the eye of a needle, and if anybody was going to authenticate the set, Cal wanted to be the one to do it. Cal not only considered himself the finest colored-diamond dealer in the world, but also the foremost authority on their various sources.

"I haven't made any commitments yet."

"Make sure you know the origin of the stones," Cal added. "We don't need any regulatory issues."

"Even if they're green?" countered Lonny. Ibrahim's stone was definitely from the Congo. And it suddenly occurred to Lonny, why else would Tom Carpenter be in Central Africa? He must have heard rumors about the fancy diamonds in New York and taken off for Rwanda, filled with dreams of easy money. There was no other remotely logical reason to risk life and limb in this open sewer. Both Lonny and Tom Carpenter had to be chasing the same batch of stones.

"If you don't know what you're looking at, walk away and fly home tomorrow." Cal sidestepped the question of provenance yet still managed to question his son's abilities. "I don't have any way of getting you out of there if things go bad."

"I didn't ask you to get me out of here," Lonny replied. No matter how often they managed to suppress their lifelong mistrust, it lay at the core of their relationship. Each time Lonny thought his father would defer to his judgment, he received a punch in the solar plexus. Cal would not give up his familial role as the arbiter of morality, justice, and wisdom. Because Cal could not control his son, he belittled his small successes and consciously or unconsciously threw obstacles in the path of greater opportunities. "How well do you know Ibrahim?"

"His father, Muhammed, is a Big Man in West Africa. One of the oldest traders in the French-speaking parts."

"Is he trustworthy?"

"I don't think his boy would stick a shiv in your kidney, if that's what you're asking."

"That's what I'm asking." Then Lonny added quickly, "Get me some information about Thomas Carpenter. He's the father of the student priest I told you about. It could be important."

"I'll look into the Carpenter fellow, you look after yourself."

"I will."

"And try to come back in one piece," said Cal before hanging up. "If not for me, then for Annie." It was the closest his father could come to, "I love you, take care." The divorce, Annie's company, and their financial partnership had brought them closer than either of them would have predicted.

If the stones were illegally mined in the Congo, Lonny would have to sell them at a "sight," not a public auction—which was the logical way to sell a suite of rare green diamonds anyway. A sight was a private auction where carefully screened clients made sealed bids for the material. The buyers never met each other, nor did they know the prices of competing offers. The winning bidder was protected by a veil of anonymity, and the dealer's profits were shrouded in mystery. Lonny would probably never discover the true origin of the stones, and the buyer wouldn't want to know. Willful ignorance is a prerequisite to collecting diamonds.

The taxi passed the guardhouse in front of the hotel as the sun set behind the hills and the light suddenly failed.

"I'll be your driver while you're here," stated Jean-Batiste.

"How much?"

"Four hundred francs a day, plus mileage."

"You're on." In Africa, a good driver with a reliable car was worth his weight in paper money. It wasn't about the price, it was about trust. Lonny would have agreed to Jean-Batiste's offer for three times the amount. The way the driver frightened the other taxi men assured Lonny that he commanded respect. And that he had deep reserves of self-respect. It also helped that he didn't speak English. If tortured by the secret police, the driver would be incapable of revealing the gem dealer's conversations.

Back down at the only swimming pool in Central Africa, Lonny allowed the Francophone barkeep to make the house special: a complicated drink called a French 75. It was mix of cognac, sweet liqueur, Cointreau, and lemon juice topped with a float of dry champagne. The master bartender relegated his Anglophone apprentices to popping beer caps while he twirled the mixture high in the air like a circus juggler. He presented the concoction in a martini glass with the drama of a performance artist.

Lonny decided to call his daughter's personal number before anything else happened. He paid to have her phone line installed and maintained, with a separate answering machine attached so that his messages would get to her directly. The connection was good, and the call went through immediately. He took a happy sip of the tart, fizzy cocktail.

"Hi, Annie darling, it's your Daddy. I sent you an e-mail. Not a lot of sights to mention in Kigali, but the weather is nice and warm. I love you. I miss you. I'll call back again soon."

Ms. Carpenter spotted him from her balcony. She joined Lonny at his poolside table minutes later. Her eyelids were swollen to the size of clam shells. Her cheeks were splotchy and tear-stained with self-pity. But her clothes were dry and it looked like she had found someone to iron them back into shape. "This Tuesday is one for the books."

"Have a cocktail," Lonny offered. "It'll give you a welcome perspective on things." The continent had a well-deserved reputation for knocking newcomers off their feet. She was disoriented, a not uncommon reaction among Americans suddenly confronted by a billion Africans calling their cultural presumptions of moral and material superiority into question.

Ms. Carpenter ordered a ginger ale.

"How's your head?" He noticed the bandage was gone.

"Much improved, thanks to your attentions."

An influx of aid workers invaded with the onset of night. They bought rounds of beer that cost more than the average peasant made in a month and tuned the satellite television to European track and field championships. Like most countries that suppressed political dissent, sports ran twenty-four hours a day in Rwanda. The expats lining the bar eyed the pretty deacon like crocodiles on a river bank. They hailed from the poorer cities of Europe: Lyon, Glasgow, Dublin, Leipzig, Budapest, Lisbon, Naples.

"Was that the first time something like that happened to you?"

"I was almost raped in high school by a friend of mine."

"Whoa, I'm not a confessor," returned Lonny. "That's a lot more information than I need to know."

"You're so steady, Mr Cushman. What is the foundation of your faith?"

"I'm not sure I want to go there." He'd encountered as much religious politics as he ever wanted to that morning.

Ms. Carpenter put her elbows on the table and touched her fingers together to make a steeple. "I can cite the Gospels forward and backward. I refer to the Old Testament by line number. I've read translations of the Qur'an. I can prove for a fact that the bishop was dead wrong. But this morning, when the children were throwing stones at me, I didn't feel part of a benevolent, loving world. It was the same feeling I had when that boy almost raped me. It felt like everything I'd memorized, argued, and preached was insignificant compared to the very real power of evil. Is that how you feel?"

Lonny refused to answer because he did not want to debate the origins of his faith. Jews, Christians, and Muslims were people of the book, but he didn't need the Torah, the Bible, or the Qur'an to tell him what he knew instinctively. He didn't believe that people could understand God by studying texts any more than they could become diamantaires without cleaving diamonds.

"Tell me," insisted the religious student. "Where does your faith come from? Because I have the sense you strongly believe in God." Lonny reluctantly allowed himself to be drawn into her quest.

"Faith is a recognition of something that has always existed."

"The conversion experience?"

"Do you have any idea what I'm saying?"

"The feeling of being reborn through Christ?" asked Ms. Carpenter. "Touring the heavens in the time it takes for water to run from a pitcher? Having a personal relationship with Jesus? God has never spoken to me, if that's what you're asking. Has She ever spoken to you?"

"Stop asking about me." Lonny involuntarily rose to the bait. "The real question is: Why would you train to be a priest if you've never felt the presence of God in your soul?"

"Because," said Ms. Carpenter, "I want to be ready when She speaks to me."

"Good answer." Lonny tipped his martini glass in her direction. "Now let's get back to the reason we're both in Rwanda. Where did Dean Addison get the money he gave to your father?"

"It was your money, Mr. Cushman. The dean signed over one of your $250,000 tithes. He registered it in the cathedral's tithe book but didn't deposit it in the bank. Nobody will know it's missing until the accounts are rectified."

"I'll be damned," said Lonny.

"You really didn't know?"

Lonny gulped the cocktail. "I wouldn't be sitting next to you if I did."

If the embezzlement at the cathedral became public, far from being the victim, Lonny knew he would be portrayed as the instigator of an illegal diamond-trading conspiracy. He could write the tabloid headlines himself: "Partner in Prominent West 47th Street Firm Uses Board Position to Launder Money." "Cushman in Blood

Diamond Scandal." "Notorious Playboy Claims He Was Duped by Church." "Dean of St. John's Denies Scurrilous Charges." "Diamonds in the Mist."

The gem dealer leaned back in the plastic deck chair. Not only was he in Central Africa trying to locate a man who was after *his* green diamonds, the man was prospecting for the stones using *his* money.

"I'll be goddamned," he repeated.

His visceral hatred of being ripped off, lied to, or cheated dated to his time as a graduate student on scholarship. He'd lost a year's living expenses in an Australian opal scam. Stones that he bought for twenty-five thousand dollars, and had been told were worth forty, were completely worthless. He ate oatmeal for months and slept on a vile, sex-stained couch in the hallway of a friend's apartment when he ran out of money to pay rent. He could recall the precise details and humiliation of that experience as if it happened yesterday.

Lonny agreed to join the Board of St. John's out of respect for his dead mother, not so he could be swindled by high-ranking clergy and dilettantes. It was an insult.

The suite of green diamonds, whether they came from a war zone or were dug up under Westminster Cathedral in London, would still be one of the great discoveries in the five-thousand-year history of gems. Their origins would be inconsequential compared with their beauty and value. To find the diamonds and put to bed any wild rumors, Lonny had to deal with Tom Carpenter as fast as possible.

"Will you still help me find my father?" asked Ms. Carpenter.

"I don't have a choice," said Lonny. "Now he's my problem as well as yours."

He drank two vodka highballs. The international carpetbaggers cheered their respective athletes at the bar. Ms. Carpenter stared thoughtfully into the night, pondering the eternal, no doubt. Groups of Rwandan men slouched further out around the pool. None of their teams could compete in the expensive indoor events that required enclosed stadiums, engineered surfaces, and high-performance shoes.

Gogo tapped Lonny on the shoulder. "The number you requested."

"Who's he sleeping with?"

"She must be very ugly because nobody's talking!"

"Good job." Lonny exchanged a packet of hundred-dollar bills for a strip of newspaper marked with a ballpoint pen. He would have been surprised if the information cost the fixer more than a call to the Cyber Café.

"Your father's cell phone number." He waved the scrap of paper in front of Ms. Carpenter. "Why don't we give him a call?"

"Are you kidding?" She glanced toward Gogo's receding back.

"Upstairs," pointed Lonny. "We'll use my cell phone."

When they walked through the tables up to the lobby, the expatriates scrutinized Ms. Carpenter's pert blue-jean stride as if she were dressed in heels and a strapless gown. Her creamy white face and hands set them to dreaming of old girlfriends and ex-wives back home. She may not have been beautiful, but they hadn't seen her before, and their open mouths followed her hungrily up the stairs. Ah, thought Lonny, not missing it for an instant: the glorious, the romantic, the expatriate life.

In the privacy of his room the gem dealer dialed Tom Carpenter's number.

"Ehhh??" came a grunt from the other end.

"Mr. Carpenter?"

There were shouts in Kinyarwandan, the hollow sound of flesh hitting flesh, then an American voice came on the line. "What the . . . who is it?"

"Your daughter." Lonny handed off the phone.

"Daddy?"

"Alice? Where are you?"

"I'm in Kigali."

"It makes me green with envy to hear it."

There was an audible thump, perhaps a curse away from the mouthpiece of the phone, and more shouting that Lonny could hear but not understand. He tried to catch Ms. Carpenter's eye, but she concentrated on the floor.

"Dad?"

"Come to Ruhengeri as fast as you can."

"Is everything all right?"

"No. I'll be in touch, hon—"

The tone went flat.

"Was that him?" said Lonny.

Tears blossomed on Ms. Carpenter's remarkable cheeks. "I think he's been kidnapped."

"Call him back." Lonny re-entered the numbers. The line emitted a continuous busy signal.

"Where's Ruhengeri?" asked Ms. Carpenter.

Lonny studied the location of the town on a framed map of Central Africa hanging on the wall. The seven peaks of the Virunga Mountains twisted like a river, marking a tangled maze of boundaries between Rwanda, the Democratic Republic of Congo, and Uganda. Two of the volcanoes were labeled national parks. He realized he was staring at Dian Fossey's legacy, the home of the mountain gorillas and the epicenter of Hutu resistance to the current Tutsi government.

A dozen questions popped into his mind simultaneously. Why was Tom Carpenter green with envy? Had he located the fancy diamonds? Did he know where the stones were? Was he a hostage? Did his kidnappers have the stones? Was he Ibrahim's source? Was it all a swindle? Was there more than one set of stones in Rwanda? If so, which ones were fake? Who had the fakes? Ibrahim or Tom Carpenter? Or did they each have part of the same suite?

"It's a full day's drive to the West," he answered. "In the middle of the war."

"I'm calling the American embassy," said Ms. Carpenter.

"No." Lonny ripped his cell phone out of her grip. "No, no, no."

"Why not?"

"Because if your father's trafficking in illegal diamonds, which you and I have every reason to believe, and you make this thing public, we'll never hear from him again. I'm guessing that he's being held by the Rwandan Patriotic Army. And I don't think the Rwandan Patriotic Army will tolerate an incident that draws negative attention to their occupation of the Congo."

"I don't get it."

"I know you don't. That's your strength."

"What do you mean?"

"We'll visit the gorillas in Ruhengeri," said Lonny. "It's perfectly normal. It's what all the tourists do."

"What about my father!"

"One step at a time," cautioned Lonny. "I'm sure his captors will be in touch as soon as we get there. We want to treat this like a big misunderstanding. If you call the embassy and tell them an American citizen has been kidnapped, it's going to go political, and we don't want that. We don't want to do anything out of the ordinary. We're tourists. Your father is a tourist. Whoever they think he is, we have to convince them they nabbed the wrong guy. It's the only way he's going to get out of Rwanda alive."

Ms. Carpenter slowly absorbed Lonny's rationale. "In that case, we need to stop at genocide sites along the way."

"Why would we do that?"

"To bear witness. It's part of my seminary training. We study genocide second semester this year. I'll get course credit."

4 That's Life, Sweetie

Lonny had been lying in bed for several hours, letting the oscillating floor fan sweep over his body, when he sensed an unwelcome presence in the hotel room. He knew he wasn't in immediate danger because he didn't feel a knife against his throat or a gun barrel pressed into his cheek. But he opened his eyes very carefully. There was a man smoking a cigarette on the balcony.

"Who are you?" Lonny clicked on the bedside lamp.

"I'm the station chief in this pit of vipers."

The man stepped into the room. He was over fifty, with a dark complexion and sharp Aryan features. Brown eyes, straight dark hair. An Indian, "Dot, not feather," as Annie would put it. His enunciation was a product of the Ivy League.

"You're here for the green diamonds." He stubbed out his cigarette on the door frame and flicked the butt over the balcony.

Lonny raised himself onto one elbow. "CIA?"

"What do you think?" He answered the question with a question.

"I'm a Trustee of St. John the Divine in New York City. I'm chaperoning Ms. Carpenter on a religious mission."

"You are a partner in the firm Cushman & Cushman. Your

father is a famous colored-diamond dealer on West 47th Street. Quite a coincidence, wouldn't you say?"

"I'm not here on business."

"You can have the diamonds," said the station chief, cutting to the chase. He pulled the desk chair around and straddled it, facing Lonny like a buddy about to deliver a good piece of advice. "We want the guy who sells them to you."

"I don't know what you're talking about."

"Do you remember the twin embassy bombings in Kenya and Tanzania?"

"Two years ago."

The station chief stood up, slowly unbuttoned his shirt, and tugged out the tails. He had a long scar stretching across his chest like a giant saber cut. "Two hundred and twenty-four people were killed. Over five thousand people were injured on August 7, 1998. I was one of the lucky ones. I was only hit by a piece of glass." He carefully re-buttoned his shirt and leaned against the desk.

"There is a loose affiliation of Islamic fundamentalists in Central Africa raising funds for suicide operations against the United States. One of them is a jeweler who buys and sells gemstones. He financed the embassy bombings. You're going to help us locate him."

"I don't like the way you use the future tense," said Lonny.

"You will set up the deal. As soon as you know when and where you're going to examine the stones, you will inform me. You'll keep the diamonds, I'll take the man."

"You want Ibrahim, the Senegalese?"

"He's nothing more than a bit player. I want the source."

"Are you working with the Rwandans?"

"Our government has a very close relationship with the Tutsi regime," stated the station chief. He moved his hand to his chin like a college professor. "I also have a Navy SEAL team at the embassy, if necessary."

"I can't just set up a meeting and tell you where it is going to be."

"Why not?"

"Even if I were pursuing the diamonds you're talking about," replied Lonny, carefully constructing his words, "any deal would probably happen in the back of a moving car. Dealers don't telegraph their location ahead of time. It's too dangerous. I wouldn't know about the meeting until I was in it. It would be virtually impossible for me to alert you ahead of time."

"Call the embassy night or day." The station chief ignored his complaints like a father dismissing a boy's excuses. He tossed Lonny an official business card. Kumar Gupta, Commercial Attaché.

"Sure." Lonny lay back on the pillow.

"If you screw this up," the station chief raised his voice, sensing Lonny's dismissal, "I'll make sure the FBI investigates every transaction you've ever made, every offshore account you've ever held, every trip you've ever taken. If for some reason you haven't paid all the taxes due to the United States Government, I'll make sure you are prosecuted to the full extent of the law. My old roommate at Princeton is an Assistant U.S. Attorney for the Southern District of New York. Do I make myself clear?"

"Good luck," replied Lonny. His father's lawyer had made sure that the offshore accounts were strictly legal and that taxes were paid on the millions invested in the stock market. The IRS couldn't touch him, but the thought of the FBI investigating his gem trades was nothing to sneeze at. Especially if it involved the cathedral and Tom Carpenter.

"We could always hold you as a material witness to an ongoing terrorism investigation," continued the station chief, upping the ante. "Imagine yourself inside a navy brig in Diego Garcia. Your father won't be able to save you. He won't even know where you are. By the time the paperwork is reviewed, you'll have lost custody of your daughter."

"Is that a direct threat?" Lonny asked. Normally the CIA officer's posturing wouldn't have meant much to him, but in the middle of a divorce, underhanded meddling might tip the balance against him.

"I'm not threatening you with anything in any way," said the station chief smoothly. "Please look over the balcony."

Lonny hopped out of bed in his boxer shorts. The station chief pointed to four burly men sitting around a table next to the lighted pool. One of them waved. "If you don't promise me the help I want, those Marines are going to escort you directly to a metal closet in the embassy. Tonight. That's not a threat. That is a promise."

"Don't be coarse, Mr. Gupta." Lonny studied the business card. He was surprised a man of Gupta's education and experience had been assigned to a diplomatic backwater. Agency officers in Africa were either doing penance for unknown crimes or trying to worm up the ladder. Gupta's presence could only mean the CIA was deadly serious about pursuing this lead. "I'm listening."

Station chief Gupta nodded his head curtly, acknowledging that he had the gem dealer's attention. "The man we want is a Saudi Arabian national. He changes his name every week so there's no point in telling you his alias. People simply know or refer to him as 'The Jeweler.' He has been in the Great Lakes region buying black market tanzanite and blood diamonds. We know he has recently obtained some rare green diamonds that he needs to sell."

"There may be more than one set of green diamonds in this country," said Lonny.

"That is news to me."

"Is it?"

"I have no idea what you're implying."

"Your man might be selling fakes."

"This isn't about the quality of the diamonds."

"It is to me. If you give me five million dollars, I'll buy you crystallized buffalo dung. If you want me to use my money, I need to know what I'm buying."

"I don't have authorization for that amount of money."

"That's the problem," said Lonny. "You want to do it on the cheap.

You want me to risk everything. In return, all you can do is threaten me with a couple of months in a navy brig. It's not going to get you very far."

"What do I have to do to obtain your help?"

"I want your word of honor that you will protect me if there's trouble."

The station chief nodded his head solemnly. "I give you my word."

"OK," said Lonny. The Central Intelligence Agency was not an organization renowned for keeping its word. Eliciting the promise was more of a face-saving tactic than anything else. "Tell me your plan."

Gupta took a tiny plastic bottle out of his pocket. "Gamma hydroxybutyric acid. GHB. It's odorless, colorless, and tasteless. I suggest you put a few drops in a glass. Hand the glass and an unopened drink to the subject. Allow the subject to pour his own beverage. He'll pass out immediately."

"Knockout drops." More than one gem dealer on West 47th Street had taken a sip of orange juice and ended the day buck naked in a gutter. It was an annoyingly common tactic in Cambodia and Thailand.

"Yes." Gupta handed him the squeeze bottle. "We need any cell phones he's carrying, names of banks, routing numbers, the contents of his pockets. The sooner we know where the meeting will take place, the closer the SEALs can be to the action. He won't be taken alive if he can help it."

"Right," said Lonny, regarding the drug with a mixture of respect and apprehension.

"You're our best shot at The Jeweler."

"I'll do the best I can," said Lonny. "But I'm not pissing away five million dollars on fake diamonds. My father would never forgive me."

. . .

Lonny wore his tired pinstripes to breakfast on Wednesday morning. The headlines from yesterday's *Kampala Daily Report* screamed, "Uganda Demands Unconditional Withdrawal of Kisangani!" The morning edition of the *Kigali Sun* shouted back, "Congolese Government Backs Rwanda!" He read the war news at the front desk while the clerks searched for the concierge.

The Democratic Republic of Congo was no more a country in the year 2000 than it had been when European colonials drew its borders at the Conference of Berlin in 1884. The eastern Congo was divided into competing spheres of influence between the Ugandans and the Rwandans, much the same way the French and British had fought for the upper reaches of the Nile back in the day. Kisangani was the current prize, a city of 300,000 people on the banks of the Congo River. The country that occupied Kisangani would control the lucrative trade in coltran, hardwood, and diamonds in a vast portion of the rain forest.

Coltran was a unique silicate-like mineral crucial to the manufacture of cell phones, music players, and video games. The thousand-year-old hardwoods became dining room tables in Europe, yacht interiors in the U.S., and polished serving bowls in Asia. Every middle-class bride in the world, of course, knew the value of diamonds. It was a symbol of the eternal. A pledge of devotion.

The Congolese government, an unstable alliance of five competing armed factions, sat in Kinshasa, eight hundred miles from Kisangani by airplane, issuing contrary condemnations or tepid support for one country or the other. They had about as much control over the situation as a flock of bantam roosters.

"*Ehh, bonjour!*" greeted Gogo expansively. His shoes were polished like onyx, his shirt starched to perfection, his pants creased with military precision. Although he was a full twelve inches shorter than Lonny, his irreproachable demeanor lent him the air of authority.

"I want to visit the gorillas in Ruhengeri. Will you make it happen?"

"Ooh!" he exclaimed gleefully. "It's expensive to arrange a tracking permit and accommodations."

"I'm sure." Lonny fanned a set of hundred-dollar bills with a flick of his thumb, folded the bills back into his palm, and slapped the money in Gogo's hand.

"I thought you were searching for Mr. Thomas Carpenter," Gogo said suspiciously.

"I've spoken to him. He's coming to Kigali on Sunday." Lonny was positive the information would be fed directly to army intelligence. He had no idea what the Rwandans wanted, but he instinctively felt the need to lie. Misdirection, omission, incomplete statements, and shaded half-truths were his stock in trade.

The fixer was a basket of smiles. "I'll take care of the permits. You'll love the gorillas. Everybody does!"

Lonny pumped Gogo's hand and descended to his poolside table. Ibrahim was drinking tea and eating sweet bananas when he got there. Ms. Carpenter was nowhere to be seen.

"I ordered you an omelet. It is cold," Ibrahim said by way of greeting.

Lonny slapped his fellow diamantaire on the back. "Your presence is a dose of sanity in a world gone mad."

Ibrahim chuckled. He plopped the green diamond onto the table. "Take another look."

Lonny covered the rock with his right hand. "Do you have a loupe?"

Ibrahim gave him a 10X magnifying glass and a pair of long-stemmed jeweler's tweezers.

Lonny sucked the stone into his mouth and rolled it around his tongue to taste for chemical dyes. The carbon was neutral and cold. He spit the stone into his glass of Perrier then picked it out with the tweezers. He carefully rotated the diamond in the sunlight.

The surface of the stone was badly abraded. Try as he might, Lonny was unable to turn the frosted diamond so that sunlight naturally penetrated the skin and revealed the interior condition. Most polished green diamonds appear brown in the rough. This stone was no exception. An ugly toast-colored sphere.

The only way to know if the stone was a true green diamond would be to polish the outside and run it through a spectrometer. The facets might reveal a sparkling gem that would make dot.com billionaires weep with desire. They might also reveal an industrial diamond better suited to a drill bit than a celebrity's cleavage. It was a straight gamble, 5 to 1 against, the edge to the seller.

Lonny sliced into the omelet with a fork. Displaying any type of emotion was against the custom of the trade. He chewed woodenly, keeping his face impassive and pushing his mind as far as possible from the matter at hand. What should he get for Annie's birthday? Maybe a CD player with headphones. She liked rock, hip-hop, and rap. Manu Chau was her current obsession.

Ibrahim watched the American like a doctor examining a patient for signs of illness. "I'll give you this stone."

Lonny swallowed. "It's no good to me in this country."

Ibrahim hunched forward until the men were only inches apart. "When two warriors share the danger of the hunt, their portions of meat are equal. If only one hunts, the meat belongs to him."

"Bring it to me in New York," replied Lonny. "It might be worth a half a million. Five hundred thousand dollars is enough money for Senegal."

"You know my country?" asked Ibrahim.

"I've never been there."

"My father is a polygamist. I am the second son of my father's third wife. He has a large house for each wife. A car for each wife. Servants for each wife. My sisters all go to school or have graduated from university. My brothers are jewelers."

Lonny nodded. "He is a Big Man."

"No," said Ibrahim. "He is an old man who will die soon. No matter what he desires, he must ask the blessing of the king."

"Does your king still possess power?" Lonny didn't have much use for African kings. They tended to claim things, like sapphires, that didn't belong to them.

"Who sold our countrymen to the slavers? Who eats the fatted lamb? Who receives tribute from the tribe?"

"It is good to be king."

"Yes!" shouted Ibrahim, expansive with emotion. "My father has drawn a marriage contract with the king to marry one of his daughters. The first brother to obtain the bride price will marry the girl. The sum is seven million dollars."

Lonny gestured to the barren hills and sickly eucalyptus trees. "That's why you work in this terrible place."

"You understand? My children will be members of the royal family. Their ancestors will be kings!"

"Then it's all or nothing," commented Lonny. The Senegalese dealer was dancing fast and loose on a razor's edge. If it weren't for the prospect of a royal marriage, Ibrahim would have fled the genocide-ravaged country long ago.

"Exact."

"If you want me to finance you," Lonny was mindful of the station chief's conditions for keeping the stones, "I need to meet the source myself."

"He's in the Congo."

"Bring him here."

"He will not travel to Kigali."

"I must meet the source myself before I transfer the funds. No reputable dealer would do it any differently."

"Impossible."

"Your loss." Lonny shrugged with the studied indifference of an Hasidic rabbi. "I thought you wanted to marry into the royal family."

"I will bring the stones to Kigali."

"With the source."

Ibrahim considered the terms slowly, then stuck out his huge mitt. "Is it *mazal?*"

"*Mazal en broches,*" replied Lonny. Luck and blessings. Once the ancient Yiddish words were spoken out loud, they were committed to each other.

Lonny knew himself well enough to realize that he would take the five-million-dollar gamble. Although the idea of welcoming a terrorist while a SEAL team trained their sights on his neck made his pulse jump, it beat the hell out of sitting on West 47th Street listening to his father's political tirades.

Ibrahim lifted his glass of orange juice. "Here's to the green."

Jean-Batiste had been Catholic before the genocide and couldn't quite get over the idea of a female seminarian. He referred to her as "*Madame le Prêtre.*" They spread the map on the hood of the burgundy Mercedes so the gem dealer could study the one-hundred-sixteen-kilometer distance between Kigali and the Virunga Mountains.

"We want to visit some genocide sites on the way." Lonny mumbled the request half-heartedly. While he was waiting for Ms. Carpenter to descend from her room, he had perused a book titled *Where and When: A Tourist's Guide to Genocide Memorials.* She was right that playing the necro-tourist would shore up their alibi and further distract anybody reporting their movements. But who had dreamed up an industry based on murder victims? "Do you know where to go?"

Jean-Batiste clucked his tongue. "Not to worry."

The backseat of the old sedan was as well worn as a library couch. Ms. Carpenter plopped into it without giving Lonny a chance to object—as a New Yorker, he naturally gravitated toward the rear seat of any taxi. Her hair was brushed, and she wore lip gloss, ready for the outing. Gogo had supplied box lunches and a plastic bag of Cokes.

Jean-Batiste said to her, "I speak no English good."

She responded, *"Je parle no français."*

"Don't expect me to translate that garbage." Lonny occupied the front seat by default. To his surprise it was as comfortable as a La-Z-Boy recliner.

"You ready to bear witness?" Lonny asked sarcastically.

"We have a genocide bay at the cathedral. Maybe we can find a relic to add," Ms. Carpenter replied with a strain of genuine enthusiasm that left Lonny at a complete loss.

Before they left Kigali, Jean-Batiste gave them a tour of the city. He showed them a twenty-foot-high bridge where children were thrown headfirst into a gully; a roundabout where the Tutsi rebels and the Hutu government had exchanged prisoners; the national stadium where the UN peacekeepers had made their headquarters amid the slaughter; a nascent genocide museum where 100,000 bodies were supposedly encased in concrete tombs. The only place he stopped the car was in a poor section of town called Nyamirambo. They got out and inspected a tiny square latrine pit.

"Four hundred bodies came out of that hole," Jean-Batiste said in French as he pointed.

"Impossible," replied Lonny. He couldn't believe it. Didn't want to believe it. There is an oceanic difference between intellectually understanding genocide—viewing pictures, reading articles, seeing movies—and actually, physically visiting the killing ground. Even as he drove through Kigali, looking at his map, Lonny refused to fully absorb the reality. To know it.

Jean-Batiste frowned.

The diesel was climbing out of Kigali now, laboring up a steep incline that followed the contour of a valley. The hills on either side looked as barren as the dry hills outside Los Angeles. Some had a toupee of trees. There were terraced fields and some patches of green on the bottom of the valleys. Yet the vast majority of the red earth was depopulated. Overgrazed, neglected, exhausted, and weary.

"Before the events of April 6, 1994," said Jean-Batiste in French, referring to the assassination of President Habyarimana that had set off the last six years of killing and misery, "I was a driver with the United Nations. When the war started the government drafted me to protect Councilor Cecile."

"I thought the genocide and the war were the same thing." Lonny glanced behind them. Was it just his imagination or was a white Toyota sedan following them?

"They began a week apart. They were not at all the same thing. The genocide started when the President's Hutu wife and her family, the *akazu*, collaborated with the extreme right wing of the government, Hutu Power, to kill the President and eliminate their political adversaries—mainly other Hutus. When the rival politicians and supporters were all dead, Hutu Power began eradicating the Tutsi opposition as well. That led to a war with the Tutsi—which the Tutsi won.

"The genocide was caused by a political coup d'état and a power struggle within the Hutu Government. The war between the Hutu Government and the Tutsi was a result of the massacres."

To oblige Jean-Batiste and keep his own mind off the hole, Lonny asked the next logical question. "How did Hutu Power think they were going to get away with it?"

"The Hutu planned the genocide for years. They thought if they killed their enemies fast enough, nobody would react. That's why the massacres began minutes after the President's plane came down. The soldiers had their orders."

There were fortified roadblocks at every junction, sandbags, and mounted machine guns, but the policemen waved them through at the sight of Jean-Batiste's distinctive car and the two white faces. Ms. Carpenter sipped cold beer as if the world beyond the window belonged to a different universe. The white sedan followed rather closely.

"What is he saying?" asked the student priest.

"A lot of people died," translated Lonny.

"What were the reasons?"

"All the usual ones."

The minibuses used to transport the peasants were unadorned. There were no songs blaring at the bus stops. The vegetable stands held a few onions. Everything about Rwanda seemed sober. The huts, the transport, the heavily armed traffic police. The country functioned mechanically. If there had ever been a *joie de vivre* in the desolate hills, it was gone with the music. On the downhill runs, they overtook packed vans spilling black smoke out their oily tailpipes.

Lonny bared his teeth and growled when they passed a group of children with their hands out. It could have been Annie and her pals. The kids went screaming into the fields in a blind terror. Jean-Batiste laughed.

Ms. Carpenter said, "I'd run away from you too."

"Here's a Catholic church." Jean-Batiste pulled off the main road into a village half an hour later. There were no roofs on the houses and no children to greet them. Some dwellings had been powdered by high explosives, leaving a single layer of bricks. A yellow bulldozer without a tread tilted awkwardly. Jean-Batiste pointed to a series of cairns and a low wall that surrounded a heap of dirt.

The white sedan stayed on the main road but pulled over to observe their actions.

"Who is that?" asked Lonny.

"Military police. It's good they're being open."

"Why are they following us?"

"I don't think they want you to get killed before you see the gorillas. Bad publicity for the regime."

Lonny stared resentfully at the white Toyota, then forced himself out of the car. "Let's go, Ms. Carpenter. I'm not doing this by my lonesome."

"I want to bear witness," she replied positively.

They approached the mound on foot. There were six-foot-high white pyramids at the corners of the church. As Lonny got closer he realized they were made out of human skulls. The low wall turned out to be thousands of human bones stacked like kindling. The mishmash of rib cages, tibias, feet, forearms, and skeletal hands completely surrounded the former church. Under a tarpaulin crowned by a halo of flies, a pile of bloody clothing liquefied in the heat.

"OK, I've seen enough." Lonny dragged his feet back to the car.

Ms. Carpenter said, "It doesn't seem real somehow."

Jean-Batiste pointed at the bulldozer. "The local authorities told their enemies to gather in the church for safety. After, they dynamited the walls and drove over the survivors with the bulldozer. It took two days to crush everyone."

Ms. Carpenter popped a Coke, as if they were on a school field trip, while they pulled onto the main road. "Are there many places like that?"

Lonny translated. The white Toyota followed.

Jean-Batiste nodded. "Every village. It takes hard work to murder one million people."

"The soldiers couldn't have done it alone," said Lonny.

"The job was too big for them." Jean-Batiste continued to vomit details at Lonny. "Radio stations were set up before the genocide for psychological preparation. The Tutsi were referred to as cockroaches, *inyenzi*. Rwandans are the most obedient people in the world. The radio is like their father. When the radio told the peasants it was time to fulfill their public work requirements, they followed the directions of the *interhamwe*. Cockroaches must be stamped out. Killing was virtuous."

"What's the difference between the Hutu and Tutsi?" prompted Lonny.

"Tutsi are supposed to be tall and thin. Hutu short and thick. But there is no cultural difference. We speak the same language, we eat the same food, we breathe the same air. It is the reason why the authorities printed Hutu or Tutsi on our identity cards."

"It sounds like Hutu Power created the Tutsi identity in order to have an enemy. Hitler said, 'If the Jews didn't exist, we would have had to create them.'"

"Yes." Jean-Batiste allowed himself a short bitter laugh. "The *genocidaires* could not tell us apart."

"So how did you survive?"

"My mama was a Hutu and my papa was a Tutsi. That means I am a Tutsi. But my mama was very wise. She claimed that she could not name the father. The government gave her an identity card saying I was a Hutu. I was allowed to go to school. Later I joined the army where I learned to drive.

"Because I was an ex-soldier, I was called to the barracks at the beginning of the war. I was issued an R-4 South African assault rifle and two hundred rounds of ammunition."

"Did you kill people?" asked Lonny.

"The *interhamwe* did the killing. I told them, 'You are not my superiors. If you touch me I will blow your balls off.'"

"Did you see the killing?"

"Every day."

"Why didn't you stop them?"

"I was one man. The most I could do was save the families in immediate danger."

"How?"

"Black magic!" Jean-Batiste said proudly. "I told them I practiced shooting flies to sharpen my aim. When I closed my eyes, I told them, I could still see their every move."

"Did it work?"

"No one ever touched my families."

The hillsides seemed less peaceful now, more ominous. Each

time they passed a village, Lonny thought, what horrors happened in there? It reminded him of Cambodia. In that country, the city dwellers and the educated had been targeted to make room for the agricultural proletariat. A pair of glasses was enough to sign a death warrant. He had visited a library where the bookshelves were lined with the skulls of murdered teachers.

The bones also reminded him of the Holocaust. Lonny's grandfather, Itzak Chalabim, aka Israel Cushman, had been deported from the Ukraine and survived Birkenau. He told Lonny about the furnaces that burned night and day. Many Jews had rough diamonds sewn into the lining of their clothes or hidden inside their bodies. The stones were supposed to buy off the Nazis the way centuries of Jews had paid off Inquisitors, Crusaders, and Cossacks. But the Nazis changed the rules of the game. They eviscerated the living and sifted the ashes of the dead. Itzak survived because he spoke German, never fell sick, and sorted rough for the SS elite. He died when Lonny was seven years old, much pleased that his grandson was an American gentile.

Although his grandfather's stories and the killing fields of Cambodia were startling, they made little impact on Lonny. He didn't have enough personal history in Eastern Europe or Southeast Asia. The connection between the unburied Rwandans, their bones sorted by size, their skulls stacked like the top halves of a buried diamond, and his own experiences, however, was too close for comfort. He had spent eight years ferrying gems in and out of Africa. Every time he was stopped by armed men he had to believe that he could reason with them. The idea that Africans were capable of indiscriminate slaughter on an industrial scale was new and unsettling.

Jean-Batiste stopped at another village. The men in the white sedan actually waved. Lonny hesitated, but Ms. Carpenter needed to pee and she hopped out of the car. She ran toward a concrete wall with the intention of urinating on the other side.

"Don't let her go alone," said Jean-Batiste.

Lonny was totally unprepared for the sight that greeted him around the corner of the schoolyard wall. Six years after their death, the bodies lay where they had been slaughtered. Hundreds of small decapitated skeletons surrounding a larger one. A fire-blackened jumble of bones and cloth in a corner. Shrapnel holes in the corrugated roof. An entire classroom packed with skeletons in school uniforms. Their heads had been punctured or crushed. The youngest children were missing discs from the tops of their skulls where machetes had sliced through the soft bone with a single swipe. Ms. Carpenter vomited. Lonny walked through the courtyard of the school in a trance. He noticed a French lesson chalked on a blackboard. The conjugation of the verb *être*—to be:

Je suis content—I am happy

Tu es souriant—You are smiling (familial)

Il/elle est maigre—He/she is thin

Nous sommes heureux—We are happy

Vous êtes malin—You are clever

Ils sont?—They are?

Morts, thought Lonny. They are dead.

Lonny took Ms. Carpenter by the hand, where she stood in shock with her fingers on her waistband. They stumbled uncertainly back to the car in silence. Jean-Batiste put the car in gear and drove on with the white sedan close behind.

"Ask him, why haven't they buried the children?" Ms. Carpenter demanded of Lonny.

"Why did they leave the children to be eaten by vultures?" asked Lonny in French.

"It's a political lesson," replied Jean-Batiste in French. "They don't want people to forget."

"It's a political lesson," Lonny translated. "They want everyone to hate each other so they can stay in power."

"It's a lesson I'll never forget," said the seminarian. "Jesus, Mary, and Joseph."

The hills became steadily greener the farther they drove north and west toward the Virunga volcanoes. The roadside vegetation became more lush. Peasants appeared on the hillsides. Banana trees, rows of tea, tall weeds. When Jean-Batiste pulled over for the last time, neither Ms. Carpenter nor Lonny made a move to open the doors. Lonny, because he didn't want to know any more. Ms. Carpenter, because she already knew too much. But the men in the white Toyota were watching.

They were parked near a small stone church with broken stained-glass windows. A full grown tree, the first Lonny had seen, spread its branches protectively over the low roof. It could have been a chapel in Wales, Ireland, or Scotland. The white sedan pulled to a stop on the shoulder.

"Something worse than children's bodies?" demanded Lonny.

"You have to see for yourself."

Lonny forced himself out of the car and took a few tentative steps toward the church. He hesitated, faltered, then plunged ahead, over-riding his well-developed instinct for self-preservation.

Two skull pyramids guarded either side of the doorway like Egyptian monuments to the netherworld. The door had been ripped off its hinges. Metal bars over the windows had been bent outward by killers breaking in. A corner of the church had a hole in it where the *interhamwe* had pried out loose rocks to push in grenades.

The interior of the church was broom swept. No bodies or bones, although the stone altar was draped in what appeared to be a blood-drenched table cloth. A banner in English hung from the one wall. It read, "No Peace Without Justice."

Ms. Carpenter followed Lonny inside. She seemed drawn to a statue of a black Mother Mary with its legs hacked off. Lonny thought he heard her say a prayer so he prayed too, "God of wisdom, show me the truth."

The room suddenly flooded with the images of the dead when they were still alive. They were packed into the chapel. Hundreds, maybe thousands, ten times the number Lonny might have guessed. On the faces of sullen women he recognized the shame of rape. Mamas tried in vain to calm their babies. Boys wept inconsolably. The priest, an Anglican from the cut of his jib, served communion wine in a daze. The ghosts gazed at Lonny curiously, asking him with their lifeless eyes, "What are you doing here?"

"I'm leaving," said Lonny, stepping over the body of an old woman as he put his arm through a crowd of young men. The dead refused to move out of his path, or perhaps they just didn't care to. His heart beat like a set of drums. He waded through the phantoms, imploring, *"Pardon,"* until he reached the light. The sugary, sickly odor of the church filled his nostrils. His throat was tight and dry. His temples throbbed with sharp spiders of pain.

He burst through the door and past the pyramids of skulls. The spirits did not follow him. It was only then he understood the odd smell that had saturated his clothing from the moment he stepped off the plane in Kigali: death. The odor of decomposed flesh, rotten blood, drying marrow. It hung over the entire country like a mist. Millions of souls fertilized the red dirt with their bodies. Even when their rib cages and pelvises were carted to landfills, the enormity of the crime could not be erased.

"Did you see what I saw?" asked Ms. Carpenter.

The reality of the genocide washed over Lonny. Evil had consumed the innocent like a fire roasting a newborn baby. Ordinary men and women had broken into a locked church and hacked their neighbors to pieces. It was beyond words. Black milk. White blood. The universe gutted inside out and its dark materials exposed.

"The old woman? The crying boys? The priest?" demanded Ms. Carpenter. "Tell me I'm not going insane!"

"I saw the same as you." Lonny's encounter with the fingerprints of the devil took his breath away. A childlike sense of vulnerability shook him to the core, and fear welled up like licorice in his throat. A ribbon of uneasy terror spiraled through his gut.

Ms. Carpenter spoke to Jean-Batiste, "How can you get up in the morning after what you have lived through?" Lonny translated the words without any additions.

Jean-Batiste's thick hands gripped the steering wheel. "I trust in God. I eat every meal like it is my last. And I pay the girls well for their time."

"It figures," exclaimed Ms. Carpenter, when she heard the answer. "Men are the same everywhere. Pray, eat, get laid. Can't you think about anything else?"

Jean-Batiste slapped the dashboard with a roar of laughter and banged his head on the steering wheel after hearing Lonny's translation. "*C'est la vie!*" He reached behind him and playfully squeezed her knee. "*C'est la vie, mademoiselle.*"

Ms. Carpenter rolled down the window and let the wind blow through her hair with some satisfaction. "Now I feel like a witness."

Lonny had nothing to say, could say nothing.

5 The Gorillas

The dusty little town of Ruhengeri sat in a broad valley packed with thousands of displaced Hutu peasants. Low concrete storefronts were painted a patchwork of gaudy pastels. The refugees sheltered under blue UN tarps stretched over skeletons of tree limbs. Every mile or so there was a water tap surrounded by a throng of women and boys. Packs of younger children played along the road like unwanted kittens. The total absence of men between the ages of twenty and sixty gave the refugee camps a distinctly hollow feel. Amid the destitution were competing billboards for Coca-Cola and Pepsi.

"Families of the *interhamwe*," commented Jean-Batiste to the waning day.

The owners of the Gorilla Lodge, a concrete bunker planted in a field of yams, had strung rows of barbed wire between fence posts to keep the refugees at a minimal distance from tourists. The grounds resembled the inside of a horse corral. Two guards, armed with AK-47s, patrolled the edge of the fence. The proximity of the refugees and the knowledge of their awful history cast a pall over the evening.

A tough goat's leg impaled on a stick and blackened over an open fire was the cook's idea of a meal. The travelers sat on the ground, their backs to the outside wall of the lodge, balancing the plates of beans and sinewy goat meat on their knees. One of the compound guards asked if they wanted to buy marijuana cigarettes.

"What I don't understand, *mon ami*," Lonny said to Jean-Batiste in French, "is why you aren't in jail yourself." He fired up the ganja.

"I was a spy." Jean-Batiste chuckled.

"You worked with the Tutsi?"

Jean-Batiste nodded. "I supplied them with information when I crossed the lines for the UN."

"Did you spy for Hutu Power also?"

"I spied for everyone." Jean-Batiste took a drag off Lonny's joint. "The more they knew about each other, the better."

"It's hard to believe both sides trusted you."

"Neither side trusted me or trusts me now! I am more endangered than the gorillas," Jean-Batiste replied bitterly. "The Tutsi think I betrayed my own people. The Hutu know I have witnessed their crimes. I am an outcast. A French-speaking Tutsi! *Ehh-ben,* the language of Voltaire is a death sentence. It means I know too much."

The bunker was divided up into a reception area, a hallway that led to six rooms, and the rooms themselves. Each section could be closed with a steel door and locked from the inside with a deadbolt. The windows were slits high in the walls protected by bars and steel mesh that prevented a hand grenade from being stuffed through to the inside.

Jean-Batiste said *"Bonne nuit"* and shuffled inside the bunker to his room.

Ms. Carpenter and Lonny continued taking drags off Africa's agricultural tonic. Cultivated in every village, it provided a relief from hunger pains and a welcome soporific for the mind. The night was pitch black. There was no electricity in the valley. The stars shone like candles, and the southern constellations triggered memories like forgotten friends. Lonny drowned in the loneliness of stars. He set out a blanket next to the fire and lay on his back. Ms. Carpenter lay down next to him.

"What are you thinking?" she asked.

"I'm wondering how they market this stuff. Is it called Virunga Voom Voom? Kigali Advil? How about Gorilla Reefer or Ruhengeri Madness?"

"You're silly."

"I'm thinking of Annie."

"You miss her."

"You have no idea," said Lonny. "I thought I lost her once when I was in Madagascar."

"What do you mean?" asked the young student.

Lonny took a drag off the joint and held the smoke in his lungs. He couldn't tell her about the station chief, the terrorist, the Navy SEALs, or his hunt for the green diamonds. He didn't want to admit that the sight of a couple of thousand bones and a church full of ghosts had totally unnerved him. It reminded him, far more than he wanted to be reminded, of the thin vapors dividing life and death.

"I won't be able to take care of her when I'm a corpse, Ms. Carpenter."

"You really love her, don't you?"

"More than anyone else in the world."

"Why?"

"I've loved her from the minute she was born." Lonny passed the joint.

She sat up to take a hit and then exhaled. "What do you miss most about her?"

"The smell of bubblegum shampoo."

"What else?"

"I'm full of hope whenever I'm near her."

Ms. Carpenter sighed. "I wish my father felt that way about me."

"I'm sure he does."

"You're a wonderful dad."

"Thank you, Ms. Carpenter."

"Please call me Alice." Her tousled, midnight-colored hair spilled loosely to one side. Lonny could see the full shape of her round breasts and chin in profile. She smiled at him for the first time of the entire trip. He felt light-headed, almost at ease.

The constellations remained fixed. The night refused to be hurried. Lonny reached out and stroked Alice's head. She didn't move. It was almost as if she were pretending to be his daughter, content to play-act and release the gruesome sights of the day.

"I hope my daughter comes looking for me some day if I go missing."

"She won't be able to stop herself."

"I'll find him," said Lonny.

"How will he know where to find us?" she asked.

"Every single person in this valley knows where we are."

She said nothing for a few minutes before rising off the blanket and going inside. The absence of her warmth drew the night closer.

Lonny locked the steel door sealing off the rooms from the reception area, and the steel door to his room after that. He hoped two doors and a concrete wall would prevent any remaining *interhamwe* from adding his head to a pyramid of skulls.

He kindled a large fire outside the bunker before first light. His self-imprisonment in the airless cell that masqueraded as a hotel room was an insomniac standout in recent memory. He had fought off chills on the hard foam-rubber mattress. He had tried to block out panic attacks by visualizing paintings by Matisse: clashing patterns of wallpaper, fabric, and sunlight; doors or windows that blazed with Mediterranean vistas.

The thick-set driver joined Lonny for a hot cup of chai as the sun rose. A mama, swathed in colorful cotton wraps and wearing flip-flops, brewed it over the coals in the fire pit. She boiled loose tea with sugar, pouring in cold milk to settle the leaves, then adding a pinch of cinnamon. Flakes of ash peppered the surface. Very trendy in Soho.

"I was up all night," said Lonny.

Jean-Batiste laughed knowingly. "The ghosts kept you company." The ex-soldier turned his palms to the heavens, in the traditional sign of friendliness and peace. "It is the same for everyone in this country."

Alice stumbled out of the bunker, stretching her long limbs. "Another night like that, my hair is going to turn gray. Any news from my father?"

"Not yet. We better stick to the plan," said Lonny. "Go visit the gorillas. See what turns up. We're tourists."

Jean-Batiste warmed up the car and drove them to the top of the broad valley. The sun was low in the eastern sky when they reached the park headquarters, another concrete bunker with steel doors and slit windows shaped like gun ports. Twenty boys in camouflage uniforms, with AK-47s, were in attendance along with the chief warden, a tall, large-limbed Rwandan with an easy smile. Parked beside the building was the same white sedan that had been following them the previous day. There was no way to back out.

"I'm so glad you made it," the warden greeted them with a slight southern accent he had picked up working for an American hotel chain. He seemed genuinely pleased as he collected the expensive tracking permits Gogo had obtained in Kigali. He opened a shed with a row of flush toilets and a mirror for Ms. Carpenter. He flitted around the dour soldiers like a peacock among crows.

"There are one hell of a lot of soldiers in this area," noted Lonny.

"Uganda," the warden pointed to the mountains, "is there. The DRC," he pointed toward the volcano they were about to climb, "is over there. This whole valley is an *interhamwe* stronghold. The President must smoke the bees out of their nest before they sting him."

"How does this gorilla thing work?"

"The soldiers will escort you to the trackers. The trackers will guide you to the area where the gorillas nested last night. From there you'll follow the signs until you find a family group. Nobody knows where the trail will lead."

"How long?"

"That depends on the gorillas. If they are close to their night nests, only a short while. If they have gone for a walk, then you walk. We call this experience 'tracking.' There are only four hundred and fifty gorillas left. It is the most exclusive wildlife adventure offered in Africa today. Congratulations!"

Lonny obtained boxy army uniforms, rubber boots, and warm coats, to replace their city clothes. The chief warden was mildly disappointed that his only guests in months weren't the Gortex-clad yuppies he had been counting on, but he was more than happy to charge a $150 rental fee for each outfit.

They hiked from the park headquarters up the nearest volcano in single file, toward a prearranged rendezvous with the professional trackers. The boys tramped ahead with bursts of energy. The sergeant carried a radio, a pair of binoculars, and a pistol.

The higher they climbed the more Lonny realized they were moving toward an isolated stand of trees. The slopes of the volcano below the park were ringed with beans, sweet potatoes, peas, corn, and tobacco. When they reached the tree line, a huge trench delineated the protected area. The refugees cultivated right to the ditch.

The sergeant's radio squawked, and he directed the boys toward the trackers. After an hour of wading through stinging nettles, biting red ants, and thorny shrubs, they found the trackers squatting on their heels beside gorillas' night nests.

A cadre of trackers had been trained under Dian Fossey and had worked with the gorillas for thirty years. They had also been targeted for assassination at the end of the most recent spate of violence because their specialized knowledge would provide the Tutsi Government with a source of foreign exchange. The two surviving trackers looked as cheery as boiled owls.

The hike moved into the upper reaches of the mountain for the next two hours. Towering *Hagenia* trees dripped with wet moss, and hypericum shaded the ridgeline. Alice hiked next to Lonny, asking him questions about botany, natural history, and ecology that he couldn't possibly answer. If he translated the questions into Swahili for the sergeant, the soldier stared through him as if he were an imbecile.

Around noon the trackers motioned Lonny and Alice to the fore. They pointed to some broken twigs and a warm pile of gorilla dung. Alice nodded her head appreciatively while Lonny rolled his eyes and suppressed the urge to curse. As far as he was concerned, the day trip was merely a feint to divert attention from their meeting with Tom Carpenter. They climbed ridge after ridge. It reminded Lonny of the Red Army and the Long March across China.

The sun was blazing hot by one o'clock. The trackers had their heads to the ground, following bent twigs; the boys were using their weapons as crutches. Then incredibly, fifty yards away, Lonny noticed a group of black buddhas. They were sunning themselves quietly on the other side of a small vale, watching their human cousins blunder through the nettles. The shaggy primates grunted at the trackers; the trackers grunted in reply. A nine-hundred-pound silverback loped over to inspect the arrivals. Lonny copied the trackers in lowering his eyes. He had no doubt the King Kong–sized hands could pluck his head from his shoulders like a child popping the head off a daisy.

When the silverback gave the all clear, the rest of the mountain gorillas gamboled around the vale like children before the fall of Eden. There were several mothers, a furry set of twins, a couple of juveniles causing a ruckus. The beasts used their tremendous strength to snap off trees, then lightly pick the tender shoots and beat the leaves against their palms. When the salad was deemed just right, the gorillas nibbled delicately on the vegetarian bouquets. It was the most astonishing display of force and gentleness Lonny had ever seen. Alice slid next to him, repeating the same words over and over again, "Crazy A-mazing!"

Lonny slowly allowed her contagious enthusiasm to change his mood. He dialed Annie's line at her mother's house on his cell phone. It was about 5:00 a.m. in her time zone. There was a sleepy greeting on her end.

"Annie, I'm in the forest with a bunch of gorillas." He could literally hear her sit up in bed.

"Are they eating bananas?"

"They're eating leaves."

"I thought gorillas ate bananas."

"I should have brought some." There was the beginning of a crack, and he held the phone toward the noise as a juvenile gorilla brought down a thirty-foot tree with a satisfying crash. "That's what a gorilla sounds like when he eats lunch."

"Cool, Dad. What are their names?"

"They're wild animals, darling. They don't have names."

"Everybody has a name."

Lonny laughed at his precocious little girl.

"*Iko nani?*" Who is it? Lonny asked the tracker as he pointed at the silverback.

"*Simba.*"

"The very largest, very hairiest gorilla is named Simba."

"Who thought of that dumb name?" demanded his daughter, a veteran of *The Lion King* movies.

Alice put her fingers to her lips. The trackers did the same.

"Darling, I've got to sign off. I love you."

"I love you too, Daddy."

Lonny realized the gorillas were the first animals he had seen since landing in Kigali three nights ago. It was as if the vortex of genocide had cleared the land of warm-blooded creatures.

He folded the warden's coat into a padded square to use as a seat.

Something crinkled. Lonny dug into the pockets where he found a cheap African-made envelope marked CUSHMAN in childlike block letters. He opened it. It read: MEET AT KING LEOPOLD GUESTHOUSE, GISENYI.

He showed it to Alice.

"What does this mean?"

"It's the name of the place we're supposed to meet your father. Does it look like his handwriting?"

"No."

"Well, somebody's communicating with us. That's a positive sign."

The platoon moved up the slope and surrounded them on three sides. One of the boys climbed a tree for a better view of the show. The branch broke, and he went tumbling off the hillside into the gorillas like a human bowling ball.

Simba roared over to confront the intruder. The boy had his AK-47 up in a flash. The sergeant unloaded his pistol into the air. Screaming in abject fright, the band of great apes bolted across the mountain, flattening bushes and knocking down saplings. The lead tracker murmured a string of invective and pinched the bridge of his nose.

The kids howled with laughter, and Lonny understood the whole enterprise was doomed. The mountain gorillas lived in an open cage bounded by warring militias. In another fifty years, folk tales would be all that remained of the verdant forest. The soldiers formed into a single-file line and bobbed back down the mountain, giggling at the poor beasts' terror.

It was late afternoon by the time they returned to park head-quarters. The white sedan had disappeared. The warden flatly denied slipping the envelope into Lonny's pocket and repeatedly demanded to know if they had had a "superior experience." He hovered over them at the guest log to make sure they wrote positive comments and took Alice's picture with a digital camera for the official website. The trackers waited for Lonny's tip with such indifference that he knew it would be confiscated by the sergeant. The boys stood in formation to wave good-bye like obedient Chinese peasants honoring a party leader. Mobs of children ran in circles around the car ranting, "What you name! Give me money!"

They ate lunch at a three-story brothel in Ruhengeri that masqueraded as a restaurant. The terrace faced a billboard-sized cartoon triptych showing a school girl accepting money from a fat man, giving the money to her mother, and then lying in a coffin. The AIDS lesson didn't seem to have much of a salutary effect on the clique of teenagers in frilly polyester dresses doting on a pair of officers. Strings of soldiers marched by on patrol: heavy machine gun teams with ammo porters, mortar platoons, radio operators with bulky sets on their backs.

Alice picked at a greasy plate of sweet-potato fries. Her knee bounced up and down tensely as she studied a Michelin road map of Rwanda.

"How far is it to Gisenyi?" she asked Jean-Batiste. As with most people who speak some English, but are far from fluent, it was hard to tell if he understood the question or not. The driver stared off into the hills until Lonny translated into French, followed by the answer: "Sixty-three kilometers downhill."

Lonny looked over the map. Where the foothills of the Virunga Mountains touched Lake Kivu, there were twin towns divided by an imaginary line. On the Rwandan side of the border was Gisenyi; on the Congolese side, Goma. Run by different clans of men, the towns guarded the narrow plain between Lake Kivu and the mountains, controlling the flow of goods and people in and out of the vast Congo River basin.

Jean-Batiste said to Lonny with a trace of concern, "What about Gisenyi?"

"We need to meet her father at the King Leopold Guesthouse."

The driver scuffed his heel on the ground but offered no other objections.

"I can't wait to see him," said Alice.

"You're an interesting girl," commented Lonny.

"How so?" Alice combed her hair with a pink plastic comb.

"You're very young to have already graduated from college, to be in seminary."

"I'm nineteen."

"How old when you finished high school?"

"Fourteen."

"How did you manage?"

"It wasn't too much of a challenge. I was just born with a different kind of brain. That's all."

"No, I mean how did you manage socially? What did your parents do to support you in an environment where you were so much younger than everyone else?"

"After the divorce, they sent me to a boarding school for gifted and talented children in Seattle."

"Did you go home for vacation?"

"The curriculum was based on a full-year calendar."

"Must have been an expensive school."

"I had a full scholarship."

"Wow." Lonny acted suitably impressed. "Did you get a scholarship for college too?"

"Boston College. I aced it in three years, magna cum laude. Didn't cost my parents a penny."

"And who pays for seminary?"

"The diocese."

Lonny scratched his chin slowly, deliberately. "So what exactly did your father pay for while you were winning scholarships in Seattle and acing Boston College?"

"He didn't have to pay for anything."

"That's what is so interesting about you."

"I'm sorry?"

"You said you owed your father. What did you owe him for?"

"I don't know," said Alice quietly. "I never thought about it like that."

"How did you think of it?"

Alice brushed a stray hair off her forehead, cast an eye on the teenage hookers grafting themselves onto the legs of the Rwandan officers at the bar. "I'm not sure how I ever framed any of my thoughts right at this instant."

Lonny drummed his fingers on the metal table. Trickles of sweat seeped from his hairline. No matter what his own father might say to the contrary, the man was incapable of treating Lonny as a partner instead of his closest competition. He wondered what strange powers Tom Carpenter held over his daughter that prevented her from branching out on her own, from living up to her intellectual promise.

"*On y va les gosses,*" Jean-Batiste tapped his wristwatch. "Let's go, children."

6 Deals in the Night

Jean-Batiste roared into the gravel parking lot of the King Leopold Guesthouse minutes before the military curfew closed down all road traffic for the night. The sagging manse was two stories of tropical wood, thatched roofs, small windows, and thick walls. Dark beams washed in a nostalgia for a colonial past that had never quite been, like a mail-order catalogue in three dimensions. Solar landscaping lights guided them to a warm yellow lobby.

Ibrahim greeted Lonny as he followed Alice through the front door. "*Salaam alekam!*"

In the blink of an eye, Lonny found himself trying to catch up with a present that had clearly accelerated beyond his grasp. He hadn't expected to see the Senegalese dealer until the following day in Kigali. It was typical of the trade, but unfortunate. Where were the Navy SEALs when you needed them?

"Your girlfriend cleans up good," teased Ibrahim.

"You want to play another round of backgammon?" Lonny volleyed. He let the quip about his girlfriend lie unchallenged. The concept of a brilliantly educated female deacon required a longer explanation than he wanted to supply to a West African Muslim in need of a bride price.

"I have the source. Do the deal."

"Forget about it. There's no natural light."

Ibrahim cocked his head. "This is your shot."

Lonny looked over Ibrahim's shoulder toward the hammered copper bar. He spotted a thirty-something Arab. The guy had swarthy skin but the pasty complexion of someone who spends too much time indoors. His short, unnaturally black hair stood up as stiffly as a bottlebrush. He wore a lemon-yellow polo shirt and a pair of khakis, and he ran his right hand constantly through his thick mane as he stared back at Lonny.

Lonny had no doubt he was trading looks with the "person of interest" the station chief wanted to interview, at length, with his head held under water.

"I'm not prepared."

Ibrahim scoffed, "I got the man and the stones to Gisenyi. You told me you could transfer five million dollars on ten minutes' notice."

"All right," Lonny backpedaled. "Wait till I check in and take a shower. I've been chasing mountain gorillas."

"Good man," smiled Ibrahim.

The King Leopold was littered with broken wicker furniture. The wide verandah overlooked the red sand shores of Lake Kivu. The cool, salubrious climate tempered the smell of musty carpeting. Neither squalor nor luxury. Bland comfort in a genocidal country too poor to build gas chambers.

Lonny held together throughout the inane check-in process, replete with a guest registration form, photocopies of his passport, the usual credit-card hocus-pocus, and a two-sided questionnaire from the Rwandan National Police. The paperwork for Jean-Batiste's room was as complicated. Lonny almost blew a gasket, however, when Alice insisted the slow-witted clerk examine the reservation calendar. Tom Carpenter wasn't on it.

Alone in his dank room, Lonny phoned the American Embassy on his cell. A bored Marine placed him on hold. A rock ballad singing the praises and disappointments of Asbury Park occupied the line until a voice broke in. "Gupta."

"The man you want is at the King Leopold Guesthouse, Gisenyi," said Lonny.

"Describe him to me."

"Five ten, a hundred and eighty pounds. Dyed hair. Bad complexion."

"What was he doing with his hands?"

"He runs his right hand through his hair over and over again."

"That's The Jeweler."

"And you're sure he's the one who financed the embassy bombings?"

"Positive."

"How did he get the green diamonds?" asked Lonny. Now that he was on the cusp of risking his life, he wanted to get the story straight.

"He killed one of our men to get them."

"An American?"

"A South African intelligence officer. The Jeweler shot him in the face."

"How'd he get the stones?"

"I just told you."

"No, you told me how the Saudi got the stones. How did the South African get green diamonds?"

"I don't know. Maybe he got them from South Africa."

Lonny put the phone down on the table for a minute and stretched his arms over his head. It was a bald-faced lie. Nobody in their right mind was going to let a low-ranking intelligence operative stroll around with millions of dollars in untraceable diamonds. Lonny understood why his father was so wary. There was something very wrong with these particular stones.

He picked up the cell phone again. "What's to prevent this guy from shooting me in the face?"

"The SEALs are on the road."

"Can you send the Rwandan Patriotic Army?"

"It's impossible right now. The Ugandans and the Rwandans have been exchanging artillery for the last sixteen hours. It's full-scale war again. Do whatever you have to do," said Gupta. "Do not let that man out of your sight."

"Easy for you to say." Lonny hung up. The outlandish story about the South African operative was beside the point. He had been to both East African embassies when they were running. The embassy in Nairobi was on Moi Avenue near the railroad station. There were four lanes of traffic, shoe shines, sandal-makers, orange peddlers, peanut vendors, minibuses, so many people you couldn't count them all with a stick. A suicide bomber had leveled the area with a truck bomb.

Alice knocked on the door. "Do you want to get something to eat?"

Lonny opened the door and jerked her inside. "We're in deep trouble."

"What do you mean?" Her eyes grew wide in their sockets.

"Do you remember the embassy bombings in Kenya and Tanzania in 1998?"

"I read about it. Two fuel trucks were set off simultaneously, five thousand Kenyans were injured."

"That's right. The guy that financed those attacks against your country is downstairs in the bar."

"How do you know?"

"I was asked to keep a lookout for him," said Lonny. "He's in the gem trade."

"Let's call the police."

"Will you forget the goddamned police!" Lonny half-whispered, half-shouted under his breath. "They're probably protecting him. I want you to go downstairs with me. After you get a good look at the guy, find Jean-Batiste. Tell Jean-Batiste to get his grenades and cover my back."

"Does this have anything to do with my father?"

"We'll find out."

Lonny changed his clothes and descended to the lobby with the deacon. Ibrahim and The Jeweler were seated on the deck overlooking Lake Kivu. There were multiple cell phones on the table.

The Jeweler glanced disdainfully at Alice. In reasonably competent English he said, "Get rid of the woman."

Definitely a Saudi, thought Lonny.

Ms. Carpenter looked The Jeweler in the eye. "I'm so sorry my gender makes you feel threatened." She turned on her heel and stalked out.

"I need a drink," Lonny tested the waters.

"Do you have money?" the Arab asked tersely. He was slightly older than Lonny. Mid-thirties, as jittery as a crystal meth addict without a fix. In addition to his badly dyed hair, his face was as flat as an iron skillet from forehead to chin. His nose looked like it had been slammed repeatedly into a cell-block door.

"Do you have the material?"

Ibrahim nodded once.

The Arab threw a clear plastic baggie aggressively at Lonny, as if the only person who would question the purity of his goods or his motives was a thief and a liar.

Lonny shook nine green stones into his left palm. Each one was an abraded octahedron of indeterminate color or quality. He chose the largest stone, ten to twelve carats, manipulating it with his fingertips.

The pebble had the right density, the right shape, and the right texture for a diamond. But Lonny's fingers felt a kind of instant repulsion. His stomach roiled with acid and his shoulders tensed. He didn't need a loupe or a light table to know they were manufactured. He could feel it in his bone marrow the way his old art history professor could smell a Rembrandt forgery from ten paces. It was a gut reaction; they were fakes.

The deal was a lose-lose-lose proposition. He would lose five million dollars. He would reveal the location of his offshore bank accounts to the CIA/Tutsi spooks tapping his cell phone. Those same spooks would use his purchase of the phony goods as proof that he had aided and abetted a known terrorist the next time they wanted his cooperation in some far-flung shit-hole.

"Let's have that drink," repeated Lonny.

"No," the Saudi contradicted him. "Wire the money."

"Drinks."

"Money."

Lonny plunked the phony gems into the plastic bag.

"Ibrahim," Lonny turned to his partner, "tell this asshole that he has insulted me once this evening by dismissing my woman friend. If he doesn't drink with me, I'm not going to buy the diamonds."

"You can't be serious," chortled Ibrahim.

"It is a matter of courtesy," explained Lonny. "Either he shares a glass or I walk." He flung the gems back at the touchy terrorist and marched to the bar. There was an explosion of Arabic behind him.

Jean-Batiste stood out of sight at the far end of the copper bar with Alice. "What's going on?"

Lonny whispered in French, "That guy blew up the American embassies."

Jean-Batiste nodded. "I remember the day well."

Alice stared the Saudi. "He looks dangerous."

Jean-Batiste showed Lonny three grenades in a plastic bag. "Toss these," he said in French.

"We'll all die," Lonny whispered.

"Nonsense. You'll obliterate him."

"I have a better idea."

Lonny gave the squeeze bottle of knockout drops to Alice. "Order two gin tonics and a Coke. Make sure there are ice cubes in the soda glass. Before the waiter brings over the drinks, put some drops of this stuff on the ice cubes."

Alice gripped the edge of the bar as if it would fall down without her. "Stay away from him."

"I can't."

Lonny turned toward the verandah. He remembered the faces of the middle-aged shoe shines occupying a prime piece of sidewalk outside the embassy door in Nairobi. They had been burned alive by scorching fuel. If the terrorist owed anything to anyone, it was to them. Six working men on three-legged stools.

Ibrahim intercepted him halfway back to the table. "What is going on?"

"They're fakes," said Lonny. He watched the Arab sucking furiously on a cigarette.

"That's impossible to say," countered Ibrahim.

"I don't need a spectrometer to tell me what's real and what's not."

"Calm down," said Ibrahim. "Gemological laboratories can't tell the difference between a natural green diamond and an enhanced green diamond, how can you?"

"I'm guessing those have been zapped by the linear accelerator at the University of Witwatersrand in Johannesburg."

"You don't know that."

"Neither do you. That's why tracing the origin of the stones is vital. I refuse to stake my family name on that guy's word. Without my word, or my father's word, nobody will touch the suite."

"You might be able to sell the stones one at a time," countered the experienced salesman.

"My father won't do it and neither will I."

"I'll sell them. Send you ten percent of net profits after costs."

"*Mazel en broches,*" said Lonny. Luck and blessings. He didn't want to sit within a mile of the counterfeit stones yet he couldn't tip his cards. The West African might be in league with the Saudi. How had they met in the first place?

They shook hands and stayed locked together until they reached the table.

Ibrahim said, "We'll get down to business."

"Five million dollars?" Lonny asked the Arab.

The terrorist stubbed his cigarette on the table, smacking his lips like a dog. He wrote a twelve-digit international routing number on the tabletop with a dry erase marker, where he could wipe it off with his palm. "Wire the money."

"Show me the stones again."

The Arab flipped him the bag dismissively. Lonny laid the diamonds on the round plastic table. He made a great show of lining them up according to size, rearranging them according to color, rolling them expertly over his knuckles. He borrowed Ibrahim's loupe, bantered with the Senegalese gem dealer about perceived flaws. The minutes turned to hours before the drinks arrived.

"Will it be 'cheers'?" asked Lonny.

The Saudi jiggled his head in the negative.

"No drinkie, no deal," returned the New Yorker.

The waiter had placed the glass with ice cubes in front of the Arab, the gin tonics in front of Lonny and Ibrahim. The waiter popped open the Coke with a flourish and set it on the table. The Arab glanced disdainfully at his fellow Muslim. Lonny watched the ice cubes melt in the untouched glass like drops of fresh blood.

"*L'chaim*," Lonny prodded. To life.

The Arab spat on Lonny's shoe.

"Son of a back-alley whore!" exclaimed Ibrahim. "Your arrogance will cost me royal children." He reached over and splashed a shot of Coca-Cola in the glass.

"*Santé*," said Ibrahim, touching his gin tonic to Lonny's.

The Arab swore again, grabbed his glass, and downed the soda in a noisy gulp. "Do business!" He pounded his fist on the table hard enough to make the ashtray skitter.

"OK, OK." Lonny picked up his cell phone.

The Arab pushed another one toward him. "Use mine."

"One question." Lonny spun the phone on the table. "Do you know a man named Tom Carpenter?"

The Arab drew a small chrome pistol. He jerked his head at Ibrahim, like Caesar eyeballing Brutus. "What's it matter you?"

"He's a friend of mine," Lonny said. "I thought you might know where he is."

"What's it matter you?" he repeated, running his left hand through his hair.

"I just need to find him," returned Lonny, hoping the GBH would kick in fast. "He owes me some money."

"You owe me money." The Arab waved the pistol toward Lonny's face.

"I don't like it when you do that."

"Wire the money." The Saudi gestured toward the cell phone with his pistol. "Or I shoot you in the nose."

"I'm going to get some more ice cubes."

"Wire the fucking money!"

"I can't wire the fucking money if you kill me." Lonny casually turned toward the bar.

"*Attention!*" yelled Ibrahim.

Lonny dove for the floor as a shot rang out.

The Arab pushed back his chair. He was fighting the effects of the knockout drops, trying to stand and aim the pistol at the same time. In a crazed burst of disoriented willpower, he ran past Lonny toward Alice and Jean-Batiste. Lonny grabbed the man's ankle with both hands and the Saudi crashed face first into the wooden floor. A raucous table of Australian aid workers at the other end of the verandah laughed hysterically and clapped as if the deadly game were an art house performance.

Jean-Batiste turned The Jeweler onto his back. The Arab's pistol drooped limply onto the floor, and his eyes slowly rolled in his head. Unconscious.

"*Merde alors!*" Ibrahim swore. "What's happening?"

"This has nothing to do with you." Lonny stepped back to the table and tossed the baggie of manufactured diamonds to the huge Senegalese dealer. Jean-Batiste pulled the safety pin out of a live grenade. It made a distinctive metal pinging noise, like the pull tab on an old soda can.

"Disappear," commanded Lonny.

"*Insha'allah.*" Ibrahim levitated out of his plastic chair with the energy of a limbo dancer. He hopped the rail of the verandah and jogged toward the lakeshore. As God Wishes.

"Those drops don't work as fast as I thought they did," commented Alice.

Jean-Batiste mashed the steel pin back in the grenade and grabbed the Arab by the shoulders. Lonny carried his feet. They transported him through the lobby to the red Mercedes. Although the driver made a show of asking for directions to the nearest hospital, the blank-faced clerks took no interest in the unconscious man. The bartender, used to living on the front lines of a war zone, knew better than to ask about a stray gunshot.

They stuffed the terrorist in the trunk of the car for safekeeping over Alice's protests. Lonny phoned the American Embassy.

"I got him," he told Gupta.

"Fantastic."

"When will help get here?"

"The navy is en route."

True to form, the commandos roared into the parking lot about three hours later driving a gray, turbo-diesel, Chevy Suburban. Two Caucasian SEALs, armed with motion-sickness patches, submachine guns, and radios, had clearly set a land speed record between Kigali and Gisenyi. The unfortunate Tutsi officer they had collared as an escort stumbled out of the passenger seat as pale as a black African can be and still have skin pigment.

"Where's our guy?" asked the SEAL who identified himself as

Mike. He was a year or two out of college, bearded, fit as a triathlete.

Jean-Batiste popped the trunk.

"How many milligrams of GHB did he swallow?" queried Mike, poking a powerful light into the trunk like a fisherman peering into a bait bucket.

Alice guessed, "Maybe half an ounce?"

Mike laughed, "He must have fallen apart like a sack of eels. Jimbo, pump his stomach and plug an IV."

The SEALs loaded their catch into the back of the Suburban on a stretcher.

Lonny handed the commando three cell phones and a copy of the international routing number. "This will give you some leads."

"We'll take it from here, Capt'n."

"Wait," said Lonny. "Why do they call this guy The Jeweler?"

"Maybe he likes jewels?"

"Nah," said Jimbo. "They call him The Jeweler 'cause he kills all the gem dealers he meets. Kind of ironic, huh?"

"Is that for real?" asked Alice.

"I dunno," said Mike, playing the fool. The sailor saluted Lonny, tipped an invisible hat toward Alice, and shot an imaginary bullet at Jean-Batiste. Then the supercharged American SUV rolled out of the gravel parking lot into the night. Mike hadn't asked about the green diamonds; Lonny hadn't offered any lies. Don't ask, don't tell seemed to be the prevailing wisdom from the White House to the shores of Lake Kivu.

It was midnight before Jean-Batiste turned in. The Australian aid workers had scurried home to their fortified compound. Artillery barrages sounded like thunder in the distance. Lonny and Alice retired to the verandah. They were the sole clients in the twenty-room guesthouse. Judging from the dog-eared guest book, there hadn't been more than a hundred overnight guests since the cycle of war and genocide started up six years ago.

"Nice job," said Lonny.

"I've never done anything like that before."

"You did the right thing."

"Is it Christian to kidnap a human being?" asked Alice. Two vertical worry lines formed between her plucked eyebrows.

Lonny shrugged. The Africans maimed in the embassy bombings suffered every day. The shoe shines' families had probably starved without them. Tens of thousands of people had paid for the acts of a small cadre of Islamic fascists. "When the CIA is finished scraping his brain, they'll ship him to Riyadh. The Saudi royal family will take it from there. He'll be judged by his own kind."

"That's horrible."

"That's justice," returned Lonny. He regarded the amazing equatorial sky, starry with planets and constellations. "Thank you for saving my life."

"You mean it?"

"I certainly do." As he said the words, Lonny's adrenaline high dropped off precipitously. He was worn out. The days in Africa seemed as if they were packed with so much more than the days in New York. There was always some concept, word, event, idea, or person he couldn't grasp.

Where were the real green diamonds? They existed—Lonny was sure of it. The intelligence agencies were clever enough to play into a known situation, and there was definitely some basis behind the rumors that traveled the electronic ether. Tom Carpenter was his only lead. The Saudi seemed to recognize the name.

"Thank you and good night," said the weary gem dealer. The day had started too early after a night that never ended. He could feel the pounds slipping off his lean frame, his reserves disappearing with each twenty-four-hour period.

Lonny tramped up the creaking stairs and sank onto the foam-rubber mattress. He was too exhausted to sleep. His mind spun like a disk, sorting the events of the recent past into categories. The colors of the jungle raced behind his closed eyelids. Deep leafy greens. Light grassy banks. Mossy rocks. Waving algae. Banana leaves. Palm branches. Avocado trees. Neon frogs. Matte turtles. The endlessly flowing river. Congo green—the color of life and death.

There was a quiet tap-tap on the door around midnight.

"It's me."

Lonny unlocked the door between their adjoining rooms. He was wearing boxer shorts. She was sporting white cotton hipsters with a miniature pink ribbon sewn directly under her navel. There was no mistaking the feminine *rondeur* of her hips, the flat of her belly, and the gentle rise of her pubis. Her wine-red belly shirt sported the slogan "Just Do It." Her breasts moved underneath the tight fabric like plump apples swinging from the eternally forbidden tree.

"Ms. Carpenter?" he said, the way a person might greet a long-lost acquaintance.

"Mr. Cushman?" she responded, as if they were both at a high school dance.

"You're a sight," exhaled Lonny, as surges of intense desire flooded his limbs.

"I'm a desperate woman," she said. Her shiny black hair was brushed and washed, perfuming the doorway with the smell of honeysuckle. Her radiant eyes sparkled and glowed like mahogany inlaid with bright topaz.

"I thought priests were celibate."

"It is a choice in the Episcopal Church, not a vow. And besides, I'm not a priest yet. I'm just a deacon."

"Then you're too young for me."

"I'm old enough to make my own choices."

"You don't want to get mixed up with me."

"I already am."

Lonny stared past her smooth thighs at the tiled floor. He took a deep breath, heaved a huge sigh. The artillery kept edging closer.

Even the cool breezes blowing off the lake could not mask the electron charge of death outside the door. Tomorrow was another day. He looked right at her. There were four freckles on the right side of her nose, a dimple at the left edge of her pleasing smile. Her soapstone skin was so smooth, so unblemished. She wore frosted lip gloss.

Her tongue flicked across her shiny lips. "I've never been so alone in my entire life." She opened her eyes wide and shot him a look so laden with feminine desperation and visible desire Lonny had to catch his breath.

"I need you tonight," she said.

"It would take a better man than me to turn you down." He opened his arms with the resignation of a man acceding to the will of fate, and she folded into him.

The first kiss was fulsome, minty with toothpaste. Her body was firm and lithe as a dancer's. Her stomach muscles rippled against him.

"Alice!" he exclaimed.

"Lonny!"

"Alice." He pretended to resist as she ran delicate fingers freely over his strong back and shoulders.

"Lonny," she breathed, backing him into the bed.

"Alice?" he repeated, shocked to uncover her mature sexuality. She kissed his warm chest. She laid her hands on his humid skin as she licked his throat, his shoulders, his ribs. Her body bucked against his hip. He half-expected this raven-haired vision of Aphrodite to swing a leg over his waist and ride him into the sheets, but she wasn't nearly that bold or experienced.

"Do anything you want," she challenged him. "Teach me."

Lonny rolled her onto her side away from him. His hands gripped her hips like a vice as he pulled her melon-shaped buttocks toward him. She reached between her own legs as he took her, with powerful pulses and short gasps, into new realms of experience.

"Yes," she encouraged him, undulating her body like a sine wave. The swells of Lake Kivu crashed against the shore. She extended her arms above her head and clasped the bedpost. Pelicans flapped and squawked on the tin roof. He made his flesh into one hard muscle and drove against her hips. A mortar whistled. The slap of bare feet pounded along a dirt path as the night watchman fired into the shadows.

Lonny must have dozed off as the night wore on, because he awoke with Alice curled into his chest and his right hand clamped between her legs. She smiled at him like a cat when he batted his eyelids into focus. The fluorescent light from the bathroom peeked sullenly from behind the door.

Their attachment to the same church, the drama with the bishop, their quest to find Tom Carpenter, the shared revulsion of the mass graves, the magic of the gorillas, the danger of the evening, the monotonous loneliness, and their physical connection elevated the relationship to a higher level. For the first time since he had met her four days ago, Lonny felt there was a possibility of getting through to her emotional core—the self she had surrounded by onion-like layers of education, theological positions, and a religious title.

"You have to stop trying to save your father from himself."

Tears spilled down her cheeks like oiled diamonds. She pressed her open mouth against his skin. "Promise me you'll help get him out of Africa."

"I'll do the best I can." Lonny's thoughts drifted to his own daughter. He would never abandon her to fate. If she were shacked up with a drug addict in the lower Bronx, he would still believe in her. His love for the girl was not tied to proximity or circumstance; it was organic, part of his identity. He loved her from Gisenyi just as much as he had loved her in Manhattan, and he always would. But in order to fulfill that love, he needed to make it back to NYC in one piece.

"You have to promise," repeated Alice.

"I won't trade my life for your father's."

"I'm not asking you to forfeit your life for his."

"What are you asking?"

"To help me."

"Explain that," he demanded.

"You're the only person I can trust. Just help me help myself."

Lonny pulled out of the bed and walked over to the windows, careful not to reveal himself in profile to anybody watching from below. "You don't understand what you're asking me because you don't understand Africa. But I'll help you, if you make me a promise in return."

"Name it."

Lonny leaned against the window frame. He could hear the waves lapping against the shore, and farther out, a group of fishermen in dugouts netted minnows by kerosene lantern. Their suspended lights bobbed across the lake like the skyscrapers reflecting off the East River.

"I've seen my share of death," said Lonny, trying to shape his experiences into words. "Most of the time, people know they're going to die before it happens. Like those ghosts in the church we visited. I want you to promise that if you are confronted by death, if you are given a choice between saving yourself or dying, you will save yourself. No matter what the consequences."

Alice kicked the sheets off the bed. "How can you ask me to make a promise like that? If death is a choice, it's my choice to make."

"It's your choice to make some other time, in some other place. I'm willing to help you, but I'm not willing to die for your father. And I'm not willing to let you die for him either as long as I'm with you."

Alice ran both her hands through her hair. "OK, I promise not to let myself die. Now will you help me?"

"I'll do the best I can," said Lonny, still equivocating. He did not entirely believe her promise, but he wasn't sure if his doubts were specific to Alice or generally applied to any naked woman after midnight.

Neither of them wanted to imagine what daylight would bring, so they stretched out the night with fantasies. Alice didn't know what she wanted or how she wanted it, but she demanded constant attention with kisses, pinches, and offerings. Mortars shrieked and thumped. Lonny directed her with a sustained vigor he hadn't felt in years. It went on for a long, long time. For hours. As dawn approached machine gun bursts and individual rifle cracks carried across the lake on the lavender gloam.

At 6:59 a.m., the hotel phone erupted with a loud bell that sounded like a dorm room fire alarm. Lonny fumbled for it on the bedside table.

"Hello?"

"What have you done with my daughter?" The receiver blared loudly into the room.

It's a fine time to return your calls, thought Lonny.

Alice snatched the phone out of his hand. "Dad?"

"I'm stuck in the Congo, honey. I can't get out."

"Are you OK?"

"Not exactly."

"What can I do?"

"I understand your boyfriend is a diamond expert."

Lonny, who could hear both sides of the conversation as he lay next to Alice, saw her eyebrows shoot up. "Why, Dad?"

"Well, sweet honey pie, if you don't get him here by tomorrow, I'm dead."

"I don't think he wants to go to the Congo," said Alice, as Lonny shook his head.

"Alice, darling, listen closely. I'm in a city called Kisangani. It's about three hundred kilometers away from you. The Rwandans are sending a relief column from Gisenyi today. I'll make arrangements for you to tag along."

"I don't understand."

"I'm at the airport. If you don't make it in time, I want you to know I love you."

Lonny rolled his eyes at the pathetic melodrama.

"You can count on me, Dad."

"I want to talk to him," said Lonny. Alice handed him the phone.

"Mr. Carpenter, what's the situation there? Hello? Mr. Carpenter? Hello? Hello? Hello?" The line was dead. "It's always the same," he said.

"What?"

"You sleep with someone's daughter and they know it before you do."

"I'm going to the Congo," said Alice.

"You can't save the man from himself." Lonny repeated the line he'd been working all night.

"Are you really a diamond expert?"

"I've been sorting them since I was twelve."

She sprang out of bed and wrapped a towel around her miraculous, all-too-suddenly unavailable nineteen-year-old body. "I hope you won't make me do this on my own."

Lonny walked down to the shore of Lake Kivu in his boxer shorts with a hotel towel draped over his shoulder. He pondered the mineralogical oddity of the red sand beach, beyond any of the river stations imagined by Conrad, farther than Livingston had ever dared venture. If not clearly suicidal, driving into the Congo was akin to jumping off the Empire State Building without regard for the landing.

Lake Kivu was Africa's highest body of fresh water: 4,800 feet above sea level, 55 miles long, 15 miles wide. Sun catchers, shoe-bills, kites, and the ever-present pelicans swooped overhead. The place meant nothing to him.

He dove in. The fresh water didn't support his weight like the salty breakers of the New Jersey shore. The land didn't swell under his feet like the sidewalks of Manhattan. The barren hills and the moist volcanoes didn't call to mind tales of his ancestors. Rwanda was just another spot. He owed neither the people nor the land any allegiance, and he knew the Central Africans would hack him the instant it suited their purposes.

Gupta had forced him to make a play for the fake green diamonds, but the original mission remained. Find the real green diamonds and prevent Tom Carpenter from being murdered by his own stupidity. Lonny was caught in his own web of half-truths, unknowns, and mixed emotions. He needed information.

Over croissants and coffee at the copper bar, Jean-Batiste told his American client, point blank, that it was impossible to infiltrate the Congo. The radio announced that the Rwandan Patriotic Army had taken Kisangani and surrounded a garrison of Ugandan regulars. Although nominally in the Democratic Republic of Congo as peacekeeping forces, both armies had been fighting to control the flow of diamonds, minerals, and timber for years. Rumors flying through town claimed the entire road from Gisenyi to Kisangani was under attack by militias personally loyal to the President of Uganda. Several refugee camps sheltering *interhamwe* outside of Kisangani had apparently joined the fight. It was chaos. Anybody venturing into the area without a military escort would be summarily executed.

Lonny put in a call to the American Embassy.

The marine who answered the phone said, "Good morning, Mr. Cushman."

"I have to speak to Mr. Gupta about a U.S. citizen in grave danger."

"The Commercial Attaché is not at the embassy, sir."

"Where can I reach him."

"I can take a message, sir."

"It's a matter of life and death."

"I heard about what you did last night, sir. You deserve a medal."

"How about a cell phone number instead?"

"You didn't get it from me, sir."

"I understand." Lonny wrote it down on the back of his menu. He dialed the station chief next.

"How did you get my number?" Gupta demanded.

"A marine gave it to me," returned Lonny. "He appreciated my help capturing a wanted terrorist, or have you forgotten already?"

"What do you need?" huffed the station chief.

"As you know, I'm in Gisenyi with Ms. Alice Carpenter. The Rwandan Patriotic Army has taken Kisangani. I believe they are threatening to execute her father."

"If the man in question is innocent of the charges under which he is being held, I'm sure he will be released."

"What if he's not entirely innocent?"

"He is subject to military justice."

Jean-Batiste, who didn't have to speak English or hear both sides of the conversation to understand the concern on Lonny's face, hissed, *"terroristes."*

"Mr. Gupta," said Lonny, "it's my understanding that there are Saudi nationals in Kisangani dealing in significant quantities of rough diamonds. With your help I might be able to track them down."

"Do you expect me to buy that?" answered the station chief.

"I need your help, Mr. Gupta. You gave me your word of honor."

"A state of war currently exists in the country known as the Democratic Republic of Congo," replied Gupta. "American citizens are officially barred from entering the territory. It's totally off limits to you and Ms. Carpenter."

"Are you saying you won't call the Rwandan Patriotic Army and inquire about Mr. Carpenter's detention?"

"Given the current state of war, our government's strict neutrality could be called into question if I had direct contact with Rwandan army officers in the field."

"Will you get me a phone number I can call?"

"I will not aid you in any shape or form if it involves the DRC. The United States Government can't afford that kind of exposure. Remember that."

"I'll be sure to remember this conversation if I do get back to the United States, Mr. Gupta. My father and I contribute heavily to both political parties. And I know at least one congressman who will enjoy hearing you repeat your justifications, under oath, in front of a subcommittee." Lonny hung up.

A handsome, impeccably dressed Rwandan Patriotic Army officer with grenades and a pistol hanging off his web belt entered the hotel. The dashing rake demanded Lonny's identification. He scrutinized the passport and radioed confirmation to his commanding officer.

"The convoy leaves at twelve o'clock sharp for Kisangani," he announced with Tutsi aplomb that would have made a Nazi staff officer envious. "If you are not ready to go, you will be left behind. If your vehicle breaks down, you will be left behind. If you are incapacitated, you will be left behind. The Rwandan Patriotic Army cannot be expected to care for you if you are wounded. Bring your own supplies of water and fuel."

"Who sent you?" asked Lonny.

"Orders from Kisangani," he answered cryptically.

"Tom Carpenter?"

"Orders." The battle-ready officer turned on his heel and strutted out of the hotel.

Jean-Batiste asked Lonny, "Will you do it?"

For the first time since he left New York City, Lonny experienced what the Italians would call "a confusion." A lack of assurance about what to do next. Run for the Congo or head for home. He would have liked somebody to take the decision out of his hands by arresting him or breaking his legs, but nobody was stepping up. He prayed a sign would point one direction or the other.

"I'd have to find a four-by-four."

"The mud holes are deep enough that hippos bathe in them."

Lonny laughed bravely. "Sheesh, I'm a New Yorker. Our potholes have crocodiles." He turned to Alice. "Can you fix a car if we break down?"

"I don't have a driver's license," she answered.

Jean-Batiste threw both hands up in the air, "*Ehh-ben,* you are both sure to die if I do not drive you."

"You'll drive?"

"One thousand francs a day, weapons, and a four-by-four," he answered in French.

"We'll see." Lonny wanted fate to intervene, but it refused. So he made a deal with himself. If they found a suitable vehicle, he would go. If nothing turned up, he would return to Kigali and fly out tomorrow. To hell with the green diamonds, the Cathedral of St. John the Divine, Tom Carpenter, and Alice. To hell with his father. To hell with all of them. He needed to stay alive for Annie.

A scouting trip into Gisenyi revealed a Rwandan Patriotic Army column of armored personnel carriers (APCs), jeeps, and cattle blocking the center of the picturesque lakeside town. Glossy black soldiers in olive-green uniforms lounged in the shade. Each man had a cap, a canteen, a uniform, a rifle, five full clips of ammunition, a grenade, and a pair of boots. It was the best equipped, most professional army Lonny had ever seen in Africa. Although the possession of a rifle defined an African soldier, very few had extra clips of ammunition and most were fortunate to wear boots. Uniforms were usually shared among the men on duty.

There were no civilian four-by-fours of any kind in downtown Gisenyi. Lonny was hot and sweaty when he returned to the guesthouse, but he also felt as if the weight of a thousand sins had been lifted from his shoulders. He couldn't find a vehicle. He wasn't going into the Congo. He was saved.

As he walked into the bar, he noticed Jean-Batiste keeping a watchful eye on a pair of Australian aid workers from the previous night.

"Did you see their car?" asked the driver. "It's a huge Toyota."

"So?"

"It is the only four-by-four worth piloting."

"How do you suggest we borrow it?" asked Lonny.

Jean-Batiste held up the squeeze bottle of GHB. "They've got five more Toyotas rusting in their compound. None of the local staff will drive, terrified of being drafted into a convoy."

Lonny shrugged with resignation. Just when he thought it was over, destiny had finally played a card. He gamely introduced himself to the bluff Australians, Reggie and Ian. Stealing from the well-financed aid workers didn't bother him any more than it would bother an African minister. The foreigners had resources; he had immediate needs. Lonny offered to buy them a round of Primus beer.

"Good on you, mate," said Reggie, a curly redhead.

"You Yanks have dollars falling out yer pockets," added Ian.

The waiter arrived with a round of cool beer and fresh glasses. Lonny drank straight from the bottle as Jean-Batiste monitored the situation.

After a long-winded Australian joke about Colonel Pome, the Canberra rugby team, a tarty Sheila, a missing jumbuck, and a rubber with a pinhole, Lonny suggested they visit his third-floor room to smoke a joint.

Ian passed out on the second flight of stairs. Reggie tugged his friend's eyelids open before he too collapsed like an inflatable doll.

"I love those little drops," said Jean-Batiste, running up the stairs behind Lonny.

They dragged the men to Lonny's room and hung a "Do Not Disturb" sign on the door. At the front desk, Lonny paid for an extra night. He also bought several cases of water, beer, and whiskey from the bar. Jean-Batiste loaded the stock into the sixty-thousand-dollar Toyota sport utility vehicle. Stickers on the two front doors proclaimed HYDR-AID—CLEAN WATER FOR AFRICA. The odometer read less than 2,000 kilometers. The seats smelled factory new.

"What's going on?" demanded Alice, catching the co-conspirators as they ferried supplies through the front lobby. She had been holed up in the abandoned library reading an Elspeth Huxley novel about coming of age in Kenya.

"We're headed into the Congo after your father." The words had barely left Lonny's mouth when a corporal on a motorcycle skidded to a halt in the gravel parking lot. The runner gave them a roll of black tape.

Jean-Batiste interpreted the instructions: "Tape an X on the two front doors and hood. Remove the Rwandan number plates."

"Let's do it." Lonny was surprised by his own eagerness. He had allowed the decision to cross into the DRC to happen to him as if he were merely a silver coin being passed from pocket to pocket without a will of his own. He just couldn't decide if braving the killing fields and finding the green diamonds would be better or worse than admitting failure, abandoning Alice, and facing his father's predictable sarcasm. The choices were equally unacceptable.

Tom Carpenter was the key to the puzzle. Lonny prayed that he only had to drive partway across the rain forest to strangle the bastard.

Alice gingerly pulled out a strip of black electrician's tape. The nature of their preparations did not seem to penetrate her mind. Lonny could tell that passages from the idyllic fiction she had just finished reading were still clogging her thoughts, just as they had once entranced him so many years ago. Sketches of earnest settlers and helpful natives, honey-covered ants and spitting vipers, the girlhood wonders of a bygone era.

Jean-Batiste commented in French, "We'll buy weapons in Goma."

7 Into the Congo

Tutsi herders drove mine-clearing cattle before them as they swept across the border into the Congo. They cracked whips, threw rocks, and bellowed at the terrified animals. The cattle kicked up a plume of dust and fear that rose over the lake like a red plague. The armored personnel carriers fired their diesel engines with a deafening roar and lurched behind the bony cows. The convoy was on its way to Kisangani, where the Rwandans were fighting a pitched battle against the Ugandans for ultimate control of the city. There were over a hundred APCs, Mercedes trucks towing howitzers, messengers on motorcycles. Jean-Batiste fell into line a solid hour after the head of the column bulldozed past the King Leopold. The ground shook, the trees swayed, the pavement cracked. The air rang with the unmistakable clatter of conquest and victory.

The invisible line separating the shacks of Gisenyi from the huts of Goma became all too clear the moment they crossed it. The ordered poverty of Rwanda dissolved into Congolese destitution. Naked children ran beside the column, waving like half-wits. Jean-Batiste pulled off the road and disappeared into a warren of tin huts and banana-leaf roof tops with a single hundred-dollar bill provided by Lonny. He returned five minutes later with two AK-47s, a shotgun-sized grenade launcher, and heavy boxes of ammunition.

Women ululated uncontrollably on the streets, raising their hands in the air and letting the voices flow out of their bodies like psalms to heaven. Congolese policemen danced crazily at their posts, shaking their fists in the air, unholstering their pistols, strutting in circles like thin roosters before fat hens. The surging populace was intoxicated with the awesome display of power. Merchants who hadn't been quick enough to close their shops were looted. Young girls ran beside the convoy handing mangoes and bananas to the grinning soldiers.

"Why do we need guns?" asked Alice.

"Why do you think?" replied Lonny. They weren't tourists, relying on the goodwill and smiles of the natives, and they weren't aid workers, thriving off the endless misery; they were travelers, participants in the drama, dependent on their wits. They might barter the weapons away, use them in self-defense, or turn them over as bribes. Guns, grenades, and whiskey were the currency of the Congo. The raucous scene outside the car windows was motivation enough for Lonny to load one of the assault rifles. It looked as if the rioting African crowd would raze their own town to the ground in their carefree elation.

The broken gray asphalt gave way to barn-red dirt beyond the low settlements. It was to Goma, Lonny recalled, that hundreds of thousands of Hutu *genocidaires* had fled when faced with the prospect of a Tutsi victory in '94. A Danish acquaintance in the Red Cross described a visit to Goma as the third circle of hell. Driven by the guilt of their crimes, or perhaps the fear of retribution, the Hutu refugees had streamed across the border like lemmings. The doctor described lighting cadaver dumps each night in a vain attempt to control the ravages of cholera. Children separated from their parents were thrown onto the piles after they drank contaminated lake water and defecated their own bowels.

Lonny unfolded the Michelin road map. It marked national

boundaries, wildlife sanctuaries, rivers, and settlements as if they were fixed and immutable. The only correlation between the map and the territory was the color. In the last two centuries the map had gone from a blank white space, to known areas of fever and commerce, to an indecipherable green. Congo green, thought Lonny, as the axle scraped a "picturesque stretch of road."

The countryside, in contrast to the town, was utterly depopulated. The peasants had fled in terror at the approach of the thundering column or they had already been wiped out by the last decade of war, disease, and mismanaged foreign aid. Alice gasped at the sight of the first body. It was a tiny boy crumpled facedown among his goats. He had been shot in the back of the head for no apparent reason. A flock of white-shouldered ravens picked at his brains.

Jean-Batiste was correct about the quality of the "road." It was no more than a general direction through a countryside of tall grass, scrub bushes, and dirt. The long-horned cattle and the six-wheeled APCs gouged the earth into a morass of deep ruts, unexpected pits, and corrugated humps. The Toyota rocked side to side, pitched fore and aft, and bucked like a covered wagon on the Oregon trail.

They kept the windows rolled up to filter out the dust and the air conditioning on to temper the heat. The waste of gas was insignificant compared to the permanent fog of red soot that engulfed them. An extra fifty gallons of the precious liquid sat on the roof in metal jerry cans. If they had rolled down the windows, they would have choked to death.

A couple of miles out of Goma, a fourteen-foot-high APC sank up to its roof in an inconspicuous puddle. Made in South Africa and used by the Afrikaner regime during the fight to keep apartheid, the APCs were designed for urban use. The six-wheeled monster might have struck fear into the hearts of black men and women in Soweto, but it was no match for the bubbling sinkhole. A platoon had scrambled out through the top hatch. The constantly advancing column left them behind.

A boy soldier, reed thin and just as taut, waved them to a halt. He gazed at Lonny with the same kind of interest he might give an old goose before throwing it into a pot. The teenager did not speak any language but Kinyarwandan. He blew the smoke of an unfiltered cigarette in Lonny's face. His sunken eyes possessed the world-weariness of a fifty-year-old.

The soldier barked at Jean-Batiste.

The driver relayed the demand in French to give up the SUV. Lonny said, "Tell the little bastard to pull the trigger."

Jean-Batiste translated.

The adolescent cocked the bolt of his AK-47 and pressed the barrel to Lonny's temple. The action was natural to him, the way an American boy might put a quarter in a video console. His buddies fanned out in a circle around the car, excitedly pointing their weapons, waiting for the action to begin.

"Tell him," said Lonny calmly, "the president will cut off their thumbs and boil them in a soup when he hears how his personal guests have been treated." The driver repeated this line in Kinyarwandan to the troopers on his side of the car, then relayed the threat to the platoon leader. The boy pulled the barrel about four inches off Lonny's ear. Jean-Batiste put the car into gear and maneuvered around the sunken APC. Units of time lost their meaning. Seconds seemed like days with assault rifles trained on their heads.

"What was that about?" Alice's whole torso shook uncontrollably.

"You got to use what you've got," returned Lonny. "If you back down they own you."

"What do we have?"

Lonny rubbed his forearms. "White skins."

"That's racist."

"You think they would have let us go if I told them we're just harmless Americans?"

"We're on a peaceful mission."

"In my experience," replied Lonny, who had spent the better part of a decade discussing the concept of America with illiterate Africans in mining camps and discos, "they know two things about our country. Action movies and porn videos. They love *Top Gun, Rambo,* and *The Terminator.* They've also watched American women degraded in every possible fashion, including snuff flicks and pedophilia. We're from the planet of the apes."

"That's ridiculous."

"You're ridiculous," said Lonny. "We're driving into a war, not a peace rally."

"I don't like it when you talk to me that way," returned Alice.

"You're annoying the hell out of me."

"Did last night mean anything to you?"

"I suppose it did."

"Then treat me like a human being."

"I'm trying."

"Try harder," said Alice. "How would you feel if I were always talking in a foreign language in front of you?"

"It's not my fault you don't speak French or Swahili."

"Well, it's not my fault either."

"Are you kidding?"

"You think it's funny?"

"Nooo," said Lonny, banging his head against the window in frustration. For a moment he felt as if he had fallen into the looking glass and Alice was on the other side. She seemed to crumble into herself, becoming more and more self-absorbed with her own anxiety, the worse the situation outside the window became. He realized the drive was a complete mistake; she was incapable of facing a real war, with real dead people, but it was too late. She was monitoring her own reactions to the horror, instead of attempting to confront it. She was a true introvert. All her battles happened inside her head.

"I'll be more friendly." Lonny tried to steady his charge.

"That's all I was asking."

The first set of huts they came to was obliterated. A hundred APCs had driven through the mud-walled homes. A severed leg lay next to a pulverized tomato of flesh. There was no way to determine gender. A mile farther there was a smoldering row of bodies. The stench of grilled, smoking flesh permeated the inside of the car through the air conditioner. Several of the charred corpses had their legs spread in a V. Women.

It was impossible to determine if they had been killed by the Rwandans or the Ugandans or Congolese militias, and surely it made no difference. They continued past sinkholes and corpses until they came to the remains of a refugee camp. Cooking pots had been kicked over in the haste to escape. Blue UN tarps were shredded with high explosives. Small bodies littered the ground. Flies moved in thick clouds, and mongrels with bloody mouths trotted by fearlessly. The acrid smell of cordite hung in the air.

"What do we do?" asked Alice, too shocked to open the door.

There was a deathly silence rounded out by the drone of flies. It was impossible to ignore the stench. Fear and feces baked by the tropical sun. Putrefying intestines. Maggots and worms. A soldier guarding the gates talked with Jean-Batiste in Kinyarwandan.

"He says they were all *interhamwe*."

"I thought this was a relief mission to Kisangani," said Lonny. "Not an ethnic cleansing of Hutu civilians."

"I don't know what it is," said Jean-Batiste. "I'm not sure who is killing who." He got out of the driver's seat and retrieved more weapons from the rear.

"Do you know how to use this?" He handed Lonny the grenade launcher.

"No clue."

"Same principle as throwing a rock," explained the ex-soldier. "The grenade will travel farther if you point it in the air instead of shooting flat. If you have to use it, aim high."

Lonny grabbed the grenade launcher. The single-barreled,

breech-loading contraption was as unwieldy as an old Dutch blunderbuss. The grenades were short metal tubes twice the diameter of a bagel hole.

"Are you going to shoot someone?" asked Alice.

Lonny looked over at the tiny bodies, then back at Ms. Carpenter. His anger rose like the wind in the trees. "I won't be killed by an eleven-year-old soldier. I'll go down fighting if I'm forced to."

"Mathew 5:39: 'But I say unto you, do not resist an evil person, but whoever slaps you on your right cheek turn the other to him also,'" she cited the Good Book.

"He meant it as an act of resistance," replied Lonny. "The same way Jesus said that if a Roman soldier forces you to carry his pack one mile, the legal limit, carry it another. It was to show the motherfuckers."

"Exodus 20:13: 'Thou shalt not kill.'"

"I've already broken that commandment."

"Well," she faltered, "there's no reason to make the same mistake twice."

Lonny angrily gestured at the clouds of flies swarming the corpses. "Quote me the chapter and verse that covers this situation."

"We believe in one God." The deacon murmured the opening lines of the Nicene Creed. "The Creator, the Almighty, maker of heaven and earth, of all that is, seen and unseen . . ."

The words filled Lonny with rage. Their intimacy seemed fraudulent. He had probably been making love with this woman while the refugees were attacked. The thought of it irretrievably destroyed his desire for her, for her body, her touch, her comfort or companionship. His emotions traversed mountains and valleys in the time it took for her to finish the prayer.

"We're through," said Lonny.

"Good riddance," she replied. "I wouldn't have knocked on your door last night if I had known you were a killer."

Lonny suffered her judgment in silence, but he thought savagely: "Gauging from that look in your eyes, you still would have knocked."

Jean-Batiste smacked a clip into an AK-47. He propped it between his knee and the door, where it bothered him and rattled, but he could reach for it in an instant. He started the Toyota and they left the lone soldier, the dozens of bodies, the carrion flies, and the flesh-eating dogs to the pestilent highlands.

As they caught up to the last APC in the convoy, Jean-Batiste decided to pass it. He waited until the lumbering bathtub went to the right around a mud puddle of indeterminate depth, then he floored it to the left. The Toyota shied and groaned like a horse as it dropped into a shallow ditch and bounded out. Lonny and Alice slammed the tops of their heads against the roof. The grenades bounced dangerously around the foot well.

"That's one," exulted Jean-Batiste.

"What's the point?" demanded Lonny.

"I'm sick of eating their dust," explained the driver.

They were each revolted by themselves and one another, and there was nothing they could do. The Rwandan channeled his frustration into his driving. Lonny gritted his teeth.

"I'm a pinball back here," complained Alice.

If the APC immediately ahead of Jean-Batiste paused for any reason, the nimbler Toyota shot around it by driving like mad through grass, streams, puddles, or sand. In spite of several kamikaze-style passes, they only advanced past fifteen APCs in the course of the intense, nerve-racking afternoon.

When Jean-Batiste saw a track that ran perpendicular to the main track, he took a sharp left in the hope of finding an alternative route. Within a few hundred yards trees filled the spaces overhead. The grass gave way to shoulder-high scrub.

Dreadlocked Africans jumped out of the bushes. They wore matching nylon soccer shorts, but no shirts or shoes. They had banana leaves tied to the sides of their heads and thick metal bracelets encircling their upper arms. When they motioned at Jean-Batiste to halt, the ex-soldier floored it.

The native fighters dove for the scrub. As the Toyota passed their ambush site, a machete swung out of the leaves and cracked into the windshield pillar next to Lonny's face. It stuck and quivered as Jean-Batiste swerved.

"What should we do?" asked Jean-Batiste, accelerating away from the main column.

Lonny asked, "Do you think we can get back through those men?"

"They've probably blocked the road by now."

"Keep going south."

The detour lasted another few miles. They finally came out on a wide track that Jean-Batiste pronounced the main road to Kisangani. The surface of the broken asphalt highway resembled moldy Swiss cheese. Each steep-sided pothole sent up a cloud of malarial mosquitoes. When Lonny tried clenching his teeth, the shock of the road went through his brain like a screwdriver. If he left his jaw loose, his molars knocked together. The driver pumped his fist triumphantly as he dodged, skidded, and accelerated down the rotten road to overtake the convoy grinding through the bush.

"We got them now." Alice found her own spirit for the first time since her breakup with Lonny. She hung onto the plastic handle above the window, rocking to the movement of the car as if she were commuting to the Upper West Side on the D train.

At the intersection of the road to Kisangani and the track from Goma, a platoon of men guarded a cell phone relay tower, a diesel generator, and a tanker of fuel. An officer, the same rake who had checked them into the convoy earlier in the day, greeted them from the shade. The officer's upper arm was wrapped in layers of gauze. Dried blood streaked his forearm. Jean-Batiste had beaten the armored personnel carriers to the crucial intersection by taking a shortcut to the main road and racing down it at full speed.

"Try my father again," said Alice, jerking her thumb at the cell phone tower. As usual, Tom Carpenter did not answer his cell phone. Before Lonny could contact his own father, a soldier on picket duty hassled him for making the first call.

The soldier and Lonny shared no languages in common, but the gem dealer interpreted the rifle pointed at his chest as something requiring an immediate response. He waved the cocksure boy to the back of the Toyota and thrust a bottle of whiskey into his hand.

As soon as the boy turned his back, Lonny retreated twenty yards down the steamy road and stepped behind a massive tree to dial New York.

"Is that you?" asked Cal.

"It's me," he said over the tenuous connection.

"Where are you?"

"I'm on my way to Kisangani."

"There is a war on," returned Cal, audibly rattled.

"I'm in it."

"What's your exit strategy?"

"I don't know." Lonny confronted the question. "Maybe I can get a plane."

"If you make it to Kinshasa," said Cal, "cross the river to Brazzaville. Bad things will happen to you in Kinshasa."

"Sure." Kinshasa and Brazzaville sat on opposite sides of the Congo River, a thousand miles to the south. One was capital of the Democratic Republic of Congo, the other capital of the Republic of Congo. They shared the same mother, like two stepsisters, but they had been brought into the world by two separate colonial fathers: one Belgian, one French. "Did you get any information about Tom Carpenter?"

"Your pal was disbarred in New Jersey for looting his children's trust funds. He spent three months in jail. Wife divorced him."

"I'll be damned," said Lonny, because he didn't know what else to say. "I'll try to call you again."

In the brief minutes he had been away, the soldiers had managed to drag Alice against the generator shed. They were drinking from the whiskey bottle, scratching their nuts. She was handing out Oreos, showing the increasingly boisterous men how to twist the halves of the cookies apart and scrape the filling off with their teeth.

Jean-Batiste and the officer were arguing intensely in that peculiar Rwandan way. They kept their voices very low, almost inaudible. The men never raised their hands above their waists. They pleaded with each other like $1,500-an-hour lawyers. It was the most civil life-and-death defining argument Lonny had ever witnessed.

"Where did you get the Oreos?" Lonny broke into the circle of soldiers.

"In the glove box," Alice squeaked. A particularly ugly soldier was holding her by the wrist.

"Insatiable Sally from Seattle," said one of his buddies.

"Debbie Does Dallas," chimed in another. "Louisiana Lolita."

Lonny wrapped his arm protectively across Alice's shoulders. "I'll get you boys some more whiskey."

"Ehh-eh!" There was a cheer from the English speakers.

Lonny gave each soldier a bottle from the back of the car while Alice snuck inside and locked the doors.

Jean-Batiste returned to the Toyota visibly upset. "The column has stopped to fight the *interhamwe*." He pointed east with his finger, and Lonny made out muffled shots over the buzz saw of the forest insects. "The officer has asked us to take him ahead to scout the road."

"Do we have a choice?" asked Lonny.

"No," replied Jean-Batiste stiffly.

Along with the officer came two soldiers. They all shifted seats in the Toyota so that the officer could ride shotgun. Alice picked a door; Lonny squeezed beside her, and the two sweaty boys jammed next to them. The AK-47s and grenade launcher rubbed the insides of their knees.

"Thank you." Alice referred to her extraction from the dangerously bored soldiers.

"You're welcome."

"Are we still friends?" Her hand rested over Lonny's hand, on top of his thigh.

"Can we just concentrate on the moment?" He refused to be drawn into her escalating neurosis.

"I let you use my body like a plaything," she breathed in his ear. "Doesn't that mean something to you?"

"Christ Almighty, Alice," Lonny whispered back. "We could both die in the next thirty seconds."

"Really?"

"We're riding with Rwandan soldiers toward a battle with the Ugandans. We're at the head of the column. Try to focus."

"If we're on the front line, why did you give the soldiers so much whiskey?"

"I'm hoping they'll be shot for dereliction of duty." Lonny raised one eyebrow.

"You do care," she said. "I knew you did. You just don't know how to show it."

The boys fell onto Lonny or against the opposite window without controlling their muscles as Jean-Batiste weaved and bobbed down the empty road. The officer tracked their progress with a Global Positioning System. Every so often he radioed their position to the convoy. They passed the remnants of a sizeable village, which had turned black with fungal rot. An ivory bone fragment was a gloomy reminder of the inhabitants' fate. The lush forest and the wet earth were signs that they were entering the highest reaches of the Congo watershed.

In the distance, a sudden movement of people was clearly visible as they dashed across a clearing well lit by an opening in the forest canopy. The boys sat up like spaniels. The officer urged Jean-Batiste to drive faster while he unholstered his sidearm.

Jean-Batiste slowed the Toyota to a halt before a cockeyed bridge, the first large one they had seen, spanning an unnamed tributary to the river of rivers. Twenty peasants cowered on the far bank. Jean-Batiste called to them in French without a response. He descended from the vehicle while the officer and the soldiers remained seated. Seeing that the driver had a short stature, thick lips, and a flat Hutu nose, a colorfully draped woman responded to his various greetings in Kinyarwandan.

"*Interhamwe!* Rebels!" breathed the officer. He jumped out of the car with the boys. In plain view of both Lonny and Alice, he raised his pistol and shot the woman speaking to Jean-Batiste. A chunk of bone, brain, and blood blew off the side of her head.

There was an instant of shock. Jean-Batiste turning to the officer. The officer grinning. Lonny gripping the seat. Alice heaving Oreos.

A wail of terror rose from the bowels of hell. Men and women threw themselves into the current or ran toward the forest without any regard for themselves or each other, like burning monkeys. The Rwandan officer unloaded his pistol with a near sexual pleasure. His jaw was slack, his body strained, and his eyes were full of lust as he licked his lips to prevent a string of drool from reaching his chin. Each shot seemed to propel him to new heights of ecstasy. The two boys ran down the bridge and sprayed their ammunition from the hip as if they were playing air guitar. A child screeched like a wounded foal.

Alice screamed through her vomit, "Stop it!"

Lonny broke open the grenade launcher and fed an explosive into the breach. He stumbled onto the road. The sweltering sun and heat broke over him like an egg. Only a dozen feet separated Lonny from the officer. He leveled the cannon at the man's neck and fired. The grenade missed its original target and punctured the side of the officer's rib cage. The man cartwheeled off the bridge as if jerked by a line.

Lonny stunned even himself. As the two soldiers turned toward him, he was numb inside, unable to move, overwhelmed by his actions. He had been vaguely prepared to die when he drove into the Congo, but he had not honestly considered the consequences of killing again. And because he knew that he was powerless and that he existed only in a dream state and nothing mattered, he raised his middle finger and flipped the boy soldiers the All-American Bird. He wanted to get it over with.

Jean-Batiste dropped both teenagers in a hail of bullets. He stalked the wounded boys, stepping on their jaws and firing rounds through their thoraxes. Lonny watched the executions with the realization that he had been granted another life, that every minute after this one was extra. He also realized the barrel-chested driver knew more about killing than anybody he had ever met.

"That wasn't the first time you killed someone," managed the gem dealer.

Jean-Batiste replied, "You're no virgin either."

It was Madagascar all over again. There were no courts, no lawyers or judges. Who would pronounce them guilty or innocent? The façade of international recognition that conferred legitimacy on the Rwandan President and his Tutsi Cabinet Ministers was a publicity stunt orchestrated by the American Embassy and endorsed by the United Nations. The Rwandans were not invading the Congo as peacekeepers or stewards of the economy; they were carrying out a pogrom against their political enemies.

With their bone heaps and skull pyramids, the Tutsi constantly supplied the world with reminders of the awful crimes perpetrated against them in 1994. But they had turned the original victimization into a mandate for revenge, as if the Jews had beaten the Nazis, taken control of the death camps, and fed German civilians into the ovens. Six years after the original massacres, the Tutsi were accomplishing something the Jews had never dreamed of: the extermination of their former oppressors.

A sign at French railroad crossings flashed through Lonny's

mind, *Un train peut cacher un autre.* The scales fell from his eyes, and he slumped against the seat of the car consumed by the enormity of the crime. Just as one locomotive can hide the arrival of a second, one genocide could conceal another. The Rwandan Patriotic Army was murdering the Hutu just as their own relatives had been murdered in turn.

It was a revenge genocide.

The only corpse visible on the stream bank was that of the woman who had foolishly returned Jean-Batiste's greetings. Everyone else had disappeared into the forest or slipped beneath the muddy swirls. If Lonny reported the incident to the military, it was his own life that would be called into question. The Rwandans were counting on the silence of the forest, the maggots, the wild dogs, and the seasonal torrents to hide their own well-planned crimes. Witnesses beyond their control would be eliminated.

Alice was dry heaving uncontrollably behind the Toyota.

"Is there anything I can do?" asked Lonny.

Tears poured down both cheeks. Bits of vomit dangled from the side of her mouth. "I want to go home."

"Ehh!" Jean-Batiste called, dragging one of the dead boy soldiers down onto the stream bank. "I found a live one."

The man Jean-Batiste carried back to the Toyota was an apparition of the apocalypse. A Roman Catholic priest, wrapped in tattered black robes with an odd rosary draped around his neck. His dull eyes seemed to have the same hue and tone as his flat black skin. Blood seeped out of his arm. Jean-Batiste laid him on the backseat and gave him a cigarette.

Alice took courage at the unexpected sight of the clerical collar. She wiped her mouth and slowly assumed care of the wounded man. She found a first-aid kit under the seat. The crisis gave her something to do with her confused thoughts.

"What are you doing here?" asked Alice.

"*Il est comme moi, perdu,*" said Jean-Batiste. He's like me, lost.

"He's one of the old regime, a French speaker," interpreted Lonny, before putting Alice's question to the wounded man.

The priest responded in a flat monotone: "Tomorrow they hacked my congregation." It was unclear exactly what "tomorrow" meant. Lonny could tell the priest was thinking in his own language. In Kinyarwandan, *ejo* means both yesterday and tomorrow. Lonny suspected that there was no difference between the days or the killers after the initial, overwhelming massacre. It might have occurred back in '94 or just yesterday.

"Who?" pressed Alice.

The vacant man gestured feebly at the swiftly moving water. "The *interhamwe* . . . the refugees . . . the army . . ." The priest jumbled the enemies and their motives together. Verbs seemed to have lost their power to describe the horror.

Lonny conferred with Jean-Batiste. "It's fifteen minutes to sunset."

Driving down the back-breaking road into a mine field, ambush, or roadblock at night was a non-starter. Surrendering to the approaching column was inconceivable. They had nowhere to turn. All the choices facing them were variations of certain death.

"We must drive to Kisangani," said Jean-Batiste. He nudged internal body parts belonging to the Rwandan officer off the bridge with his toe. He kicked the body of the second boy soldier into the stream, where it bobbed and rolled like a carp.

"We'll be ambushed by the Ugandans."

"Then our trip will end quickly."

They both chuckled uncomfortably at the macabre joke. A fast demise would release them from the torture of further choices.

"What shall we do?" Lonny consulted Alice. "Try to reach your father or turn back?"

"I can't make that decision," replied Alice. "You make it for me."

"OK," said Lonny, taking matters into his own hands. "Kisangani or bust."

"It will take the night," replied Jean-Batiste. He removed metal jerry cans of fuel from the roof and poured them into the thirsty gas tank.

They clamored into the rugged Toyota. The deacon and the priest comforted each other in the rear. Jean-Batiste drove. Lonny was armed and dismayed in the passenger seat. If they were shot at, it was unlikely he would have the opportunity to return fire. The assault rifle functioned as a placebo, reassuring him but useless. The sun soon snuffed itself out against the treetops. Their headlights bumped down the disintegrating road, poking lost beams into the gloom.

The infinite dark grew more terrifying the farther they ventured into its reaches. Eventually the night enveloped them as tightly as the belly of a snake. They couldn't see the stars above, the trees to the right or left, not even the path behind them. They couldn't have been more alone or lonely in the outer reaches of space.

They turned on the overhead light just so they could see each other.

"Tell the Father I'm going to be a priest too," said Alice, holding the hand of the wounded padre. "Ask him what he thinks about that."

Lonny took his time relaying the information in French, along with some background about Alice, the Anglican church, and the original reason for their journey. Jean-Batiste listened closely.

The priest unexpectedly put his free hand over Ms. Carpenter's. "I hope your sex is the future of a new institution. The people have lost the ability to tell right from wrong. They need guidance but they cannot accept it after what has been done in the name of the church. Maybe you and your daughters can bring it back again."

Lonny translated the remark and Alice burst out, "I don't know where to begin!"

"God has prepared you for this task," replied the priest. "You must not live for yourself but for others. You may think God has abandoned you because you have suffered unimaginable cruelty. You must ask yourself, 'How may I serve the people?'"

"It's easy for a priest," Jean-Batiste blurted. "What about a soldier? Am I supposed to serve the Tutsi regime? They are more wicked than Hutu Power."

The priest lost interest. "You must serve your conscience."

"After the genocide," confessed Jean-Batiste, "I helped the Rwandan Patriotic Army execute the *interhamwe*. I thought, God will never punish them."

"How many?" asked Lonny.

"I had two hundred rounds."

"You killed two hundred men?"

"Men, women . . ."

The priest said nothing. He had obviously heard it before. What was new between people and death? He must have seen so many ditches filled with bodies that he no longer regarded the living as much more than talking dust. Lonny realized the rosary around the priest's neck was fashioned out of human finger bones. The night stretched without end.

Alice guessed something of Jean-Batiste's French confession, for she said, "I had an abortion." Lonny didn't translate that remark. He felt there was a vast oceanic expanse of interpretation between a fetus and a baby, self-defense and murder. Was self-defense murder? Was abortion self-defense?

When Annie was conceived during a January romp in the Bahamas, Lonny urged his date to have an abortion. Cass resisted. He married the woman to give his daughter a father, and he loved the role. Annie had become the most wonderful person he had ever met. But he had always worried that being yoked to Cass would end "in laments," as his grandfather was fond of saying.

Cass knew that he objected to her, not Annie, but she often fell back on the original argument over the abortion as if her refusal conferred upon her an irrefutable proof of maternal love. She had not graduated from college. She had never held a steady job. Giving birth was the biggest accomplishment of her life. She trotted out Annie like a pedigreed poodle, plotting her daycare, kindergarten, and grade school acceptances like a campaign to win Best in Show at Madison Square Garden. Cass laid claim to Annie's fine character and disowned the normal outbursts of rebellion as being "just like your dammed father."

Lonny said to Alice, "I don't think an abortion is such a big deal."

"A Roman Catholic would."

"Why beat yourself up?"

Alice waved her hands in a circle. "I want everyone to know what I've done."

"If it wasn't for your father, you wouldn't be here."

"Don't bring my father into it."

"Why not?"

"I think he may have killed us."

Jean-Batiste lit a cigarette, and the Catholic priest mumbled while he fingered the bones of his former parishioners. The blackness tightened its grip after midnight. Swarms of insects pattered against the windshield like raindrops. The ghost-road linking the rain forest to Kisangani was as empty as the Sahara.

They passed through one good-sized town at a river junction. The lights, if there had been any, were mute. Nobody prevented them from crossing the bridge. Even the animals were silent. It seemed as if they were the last survivors of a biological war that had ended the human race.

They were each alone together. Lonny had cowered several hours on an airport tarmac in Angola waiting for a chartered plane while mortars rained down. He had sat on a toilet seat in Cambodia holding the door shut with his legs as a gang of pimps promised to slice off his dick. He had fled twenty miles through the bush in Madagascar by the light of the moon. None of it compared with the elephantine terror that seized him now. His skin crawled, his ears rang, his eyes wept from the strain. They bounced from pothole to pothole, descending ever farther into the void, from tarmac to laterite, as he waited for a land mine to blow off his legs or a bullet to shatter the glass membrane separating him from oblivion.

The insanity of the visible darkness brought to mind his mother and her madness, descending, perhaps rising, closing in around her as she lost the ability to stay the course. She would have taken Lonny with her, like an ancient queen whose servants accompany her to the netherworld, if she had not lost track of time altogether and jumped to her death before he arrived home from school. He experienced the night through her eyes now, that inability to comprehend the nature of the ominous gloom as it pushed in on all sides.

The absolute terror of the velveteen Congolese night did not compare to anything he had yet survived. The darkness was as thick and pungent as a serpent's bowels, alive, vibrating with energy, beyond comprehension. He understood why it had reduced generations of Africans to mental slavery, forcing them to rely on the intervention of sorcerers to placate the abiding evil.

When he closed his eyes, he involuntarily pictured the impact of the grenade as it entered the Rwandan officer's chest. The man's bloodshot eyes bulged out for a fraction of a second as the missile knocked him over the edge. The black face and its green uniform tumbled into the muddy water so fast even the boy soldiers were surprised. And he remembered the sight of Jean-Batiste's rounds tearing into them. How could he ask for forgiveness a second time? He had killed in Madagascar and now he had killed again.

During the middle watch, those small hours between midnight and four a.m. that deep-sea sailors prize, he finally laid his starving soul alongside God's. He knew that he was powerless to save his own life and the lives of those around him. He realized that he was no more able to change his destiny than the endangered gorillas plucking leaves on their forlorn mountaintop. If he made it down the nightmare highway it would be a miracle equal to that of his grandfather surviving Birkenau. There wasn't a teardrop of pride left in the gem dealer, not a carat weight of light. He cradled the dead star of his soul in his lap like a condemned man rocking to the executioner's whetstone.

His love for Annie was the only redeeming quality of his squandered, nihilistic existence. His liaison with Alice had been little more than an attempt to placate the cancer of emptiness gnawing at his worst hours. With nothing left to lose, he made the feeble decision to pit his last mustard seed of faith against the darkness. He begged God Almighty to accept him as he was. A sinner.

Although dawn's rosy cheeks were slow in coming to that battered Japanese chariot, Lonny eventually spelled Jean-Batiste at the wheel and laughed at a nightjar that banged into the windshield. His heart was singing by the time they reached the first roadblock of the morning. Love was the answer. The hope, the reward. Its faded imprint led him through the night like the memory of his mother's lips on his forehead.

8 A Fistful of Diamonds

On any other day of his life, Lonny would have jammed the Toyota into reverse and accelerated backward at the sight of a small string of stones arranged across the road and an oozing berm of bodies nestled to the side. But the terrors of the night had driven the gem dealer so far over the edge of the breaking point and back that the spectacle of his fellow human beings, some high on drugs, others gesticulating madly, all boot-black Africans with pus-colored eyes and trembling fingers on their worn triggers, was a welcome relief.

He braked next to the pile of bloated and blistering corpses. The vacant orbs of the dead regarded him with indifference. The smell overwhelmed the senses: a pungent blend of sugary flesh, putrefaction, and despair. Odd hands poked out of the mass. Lonny could not tell at a glance if the soldiers controlling the checkpoint were Ugandan or Rwandan. Apparently Jean-Batiste couldn't either, because he stared hard through the windshield without saying a word. Lonny stepped out of the Toyota and approached the heavily armed soldiers.

"*Hodi!*" exclaimed Lonny. It was a Swahili word traditionally used in much of East Africa before entering somebody's house. It wasn't French or English; it wasn't Kinyarwandan or one of the twelve tribal dialects spoken in Uganda. It was an absolutely bizarre word choice, and he hoped neutral. A linguistic blunder would get them all killed before they had a chance to negotiate.

"*Karibou*," a soldier replied with the traditional Swahili welcome.

Another soldier, with a black do-rag, ammunition belts looped over his left shoulder, and a .30 caliber machine gun balanced in his right hand, sprang forward like an action hero and fired a deafening burst of gunfire over Lonny's head. The fighter shouted in Kinyarwandan.

Jean-Batiste stuck his head out the car window and swore at his fellow Rwandans as only an ex-sergeant can. The Tutsi soldiers howled with laughter at the crestfallen fighter with the machine gun. Lonny was saved again. It was surreal, mentally living and dying like that while his body remained unscathed.

They had made it through the forest to Kisangani—the largest city in the eastern Congo, battleground between the Ugandans and Rwandans, and the last known location of one Thomas Carpenter. Lonny prayed that the man was still alive; he felt he deserved at least that much.

There were handshakes all around with the news that the Toyota was the first element of the relief column coming from Gisenyi. The Tutsi soldiers were properly awed when Jean-Batiste showed them a charm he had used to ward off the seven thousand devils of the forest. He narrated their trip and claimed the dried bugs on the hood belonged to the belch of a gigantic toad. Surely no one else had driven down that track after sunset and lived to tell it. Five cases of beer and the remaining whiskey sealed the soldiers' cooperation.

The radio crackled back and forth until the travelers were escorted from the roadblock through a dozen others toward a Catholic mission. Diamonds and death seemed to be the only two viable businesses. One hut had a sign that read, "Mr. Cash" next to a crudely stenciled diamond. Others said, "The Terminator's Big Diamond Emporium," "The Cash Cow," "Scud Missile Diamonds," "Diamonds

For Now," and "Love Diamonds Baby." Rows of newly finished coffins were propped open for inspection next to carpentry shops.

Each roadblock mimicked the first, a series of pebbles accompanied by a pile of bodies. The most serious checkpoints had trenched machine gun emplacements, crossing fields of fire and minefields. The Rwandans were expecting attacks from the Ugandan-backed native militias. The ranks of the militias were filled with drugged teenage boys who ran fearlessly up the road yelling *"maji, maji, maji"* under the unfortunate delusion that the Swahili word for water would turn the Rwandan lead into rain. A local militia had lured a United Nations observer from Morocco into the forest and ritually cannibalized him the previous week.

Kisangani could only be described as the graveyard of hope, a sprawling mud pit beside the River Congo trampled by greed. It was here East met West astride the impassable falls in the 1800s: the farthest navigable station up the river from the Kongo people on the Atlantic Ocean, the farthest inland trading post controlled by the Sultan of Zanzibar on the Indian Ocean. After two centuries of supplying ivory, slaves, and religious converts to the world, it remained a vast, fetid slum.

Cités of shacks with corrugated roofs and wooden walls leaned against each other for support. An occasional concrete building peppered with bullet holes broke the monotony. The streets were paved with fish bones and fruit skins. The only relics of nineteenth- and twentieth-century contact with the outside world were a row of flamboyant trees imported from the Caribbean and six frozen cranes hovering over the vacant quays. Barges that plied the thirteen hundred river miles between Kinshasa, located above the first major set of cataracts near the coast, and Kisangani, built below the second impassable cataract, had stopped running years ago.

Every once in a while there was the thump, whistle, and blast of a mortar shell flying from one section of the misery toward the other as the Ugandans and the Rwandans punished the populace for not supporting their respective armies.

Their Rwandan escort, another Tutsi boy with a bayonet fixed on the end of his assault rifle, directed them away from the bend in the river down a complicated series of alleys toward a dirty airport at the outskirts of habitation. An entirely naked man, his body covered in gray ash, threw a rock at the Toyota. Crowds of AIDS orphans streaked beside the car begging hysterically. Half-naked women carrying buckets of water on their heads gestured weakly. Lonny realized the HYDR-AID stickers on the outside of the vehicle were drawing the inhabitants toward the sport utility vehicle like bees to honey.

Alice gave out a fistful of penny candy and a bottle of water at one checkpoint. The sweets went into the children's mouths before they were spit back out again and shared with the others. The plastic bottle became the center of a fistfight.

"I've never seen anything like it," said Jean-Batiste, a forty-five-year-old who had lived as both a Hutu and a Tutsi through four genocides. "The women don't have enough fabric to cover their breasts."

They accelerated away from the children fast enough to arrive at the Catholic mission without the frantic mob. The compound walls were charred by grenade blasts.

Lonny banged on the door of the clinic.

"Go away," came a shout in French from the other side of the door.

"There is a priest to see you!"

The metal gate scraped open an inch. The fat face of an African nun greeted Lonny with a disapproving frown. "We must conserve our resources."

"I have a holy father in the car."

She cracked the gate open and waddled over to the car. "Father Celestin!"

The priest closed his eyes. There was a great fuss as black nuns poured out of the mission at the Mother Superior's screech.

"Good-bye," said Alice.

The priest squeezed her hand. They carried him into the mission and locked the metal gate without offering sanctuary.

"We were the most Catholic country in Africa before the genocide," said Jean-Batiste sadly. "The Pope came to Kigali twice."

"What happened?"

Jean-Batiste gestured lamely at the closed gate. "They lost faith in us."

It was another heart-squeezing ride through acres of feces and rotting human beings to the airport. An albino woman dragged a child by the heel across the waste. Giant scorched wheels, aluminum wings, and mangled tail sections were souvenirs of past air disasters. One section of broken fuselage housed a donkey.

The airport terminal was nothing less than a fortified command post. The roof bristled with antennas and satellite dishes. Snipers peered down behind sandbags. The control tower loomed like a medieval turret. Deep trenches, earthen mounds, and concertina wire surrounded the castle-like walls.

Tom Carpenter waved at them as they pulled into the parking lot. He was in his early fifties. His narrow face was framed by distinguished gray locks and sideburns. He could have easily mixed with the legions of commuters who rode Metro North from Connecticut to Wall Street everyday. Trim, neat, confidence-inspiring.

"Dad!" Ms. Carpenter leapt from the car.

"Alice!" They hugged each other tightly. Lonny couldn't help thinking of Annie. A guard noted the touching father-daughter reunion by hawking a tubercular gob of phlegm.

"We nearly died," said Alice.

"Thank God you're here."

"I have so much to ask you."

"Not now, pumpkin," her father replied, indicating a military officer with a sideways nod.

Lonny appraised Tom Carpenter with a jaundiced eye as a hot layer of sweat coated his body.

"You must be the diamantaire." Tom Carpenter turned to Lonny. "You don't know how glad I am to see you."

"I can guess."

"I suppose you'll want to meet the Big Man." Tom said it grandly, as if the gem dealer had been invited to meet a political candidate.

"What the hell is going on?"

"I've been a hostage for weeks—" started Tom.

"General Kegama awaits," bellowed an officer with gold-rimmed glasses, a gold watch, a gold pen, a gold necklace, and gold epaulets. He confiscated their weapons and their foreign passports. He muttered Kinyarwandan death threats to Jean-Batiste, ordering the driver to park the car in the hot sun away from the entrance. He pushed the whites into the sweltering terminal. Staff officers sneered at their pale faces as they walked by.

Lonny was surprised to hear the officers speaking English, until he remembered that all the original officers in the Rwandan Patriotic Army had been drawn from Ugandan army. The President of Rwanda had once been the head of Uganda's intelligence service.

"I eat *mzungu* for breakfast," taunted a colonel with silver braid on his hat. It was not funny: eating whites as a meal. The gold-plated officer led them down an unpainted hallway reeking of urine. He knocked sharply on a closed door.

"Enter," commanded the voice.

General Kegama sat behind a desk with a variety of cell phones laid out in rows. Tall and blade-like, he radiated an air of Prussian authority. He licked his lips dryly at the sight of the New York diamantaire.

"Come with me," he ordered with a clipped American accent. He opened another door at the rear of the room and marched down a filthy corridor to a cinder-block room. There were four long, rectangular tables and a row of glass-slatted windows facing the tarmac.

"Your reputation precedes you, Mr. Cushman," said the general, tossing a diamond crystal onto a table.

Lonny picked the stone off the table and held it to the light. "Who told you I was a diamantaire?"

General Kegama clucked his tongue. "Don't play me for a fool. I was trained in Mounted Armor Command Doctrine at Fort Knox. I understand Americans better than most, Mr. Cushman."

"I am on a mission of peace." Lonny stuck to his cover story as he indicated Alice with an open palm. "I think there has been a huge misunderstanding."

"What is your association with Mr. Carpenter?"

Lonny looked over at Tom, who had gone stiff with fear.

"I have no association with Mr. Carpenter. As far as I am aware he's just a tourist. I am a member of the board of trustees of the Cathedral of St. John the Divine in New York City, in obedience to the Protestant Episcopal Church of America, a member of the worldwide Anglican Communion, under the spiritual authority of the Archbishop of Canterbury. I have agreed to accompany Ms. Alice Carpenter as part of my wider duty to the church. We're here to retrieve her father."

"Do you know why I have placed Mr. Carpenter in detention?" asked the general rhetorically. "Because he is a thief. He came to Kisangani to purchase diamonds from the Ugandans," the general slammed his hand down on the table, "when he knew it was against international law. The Rwandan Patriotic Army has been tasked with the maintenance of peace and stability in the Eastern Congo. We have a mandate from the President of the Democratic Republic of Congo. We are recognized by the United Nations as a legitimate peacekeeping force. The Ugandans are profiteering mercenaries. Mr. Thomas Carpenter aided the enemy. I am within my rights to chop him."

"I honestly didn't know," said Tom Carpenter. "I swear."

"Shut up!" snapped the general.

"Please have mercy," pleaded Alice.

The general narrowed his eyes at the female deacon.

"What do you want from me?" asked Lonny, as Alice put her hand on her father's arm.

General Kegama breathed in through his nose. "Six weeks ago I launched attacks aimed at bringing a halt to the diamond trade and preventing the Ugandans from using their ill-gotten gains to purchase weapons. I closed the *comptoirs*. I seized the entire diamond inventory of the city. Unfortunately, I did not arrest the dealers. The Ugandans capitalized on my error. They kidnapped every capable diamantaire in Kisangani. Mr. Carpenter volunteered his services to me shortly afterward, but he is totally incompetent.

"I have been following your every move, Mr. Cushman, since you stepped off the plane in Kigali. I am the one who instructed Mr. Carpenter to lead you to Ruhengeri. I sent you the note on the mountaintop. I instructed my aide to meet you in Gisenyi and escort you here."

"We lost him in the forest," said Lonny. A bottomless pit opened deep in the center of his being. While he thought he was pursuing Tom Carpenter and the green diamonds, the general had been manipulating him like a puppeteer. From the instant Lonny had touched down in Kigali he had become the prey, not the predator.

"You are going to sort the stones for me," the general commented.

"Why?"

"It's none of your concern."

"If you don't tell me, I can't do the job."

"I'll kill you."

"Who will sort the stones?"

The general coughed into the air.

Lonny interpreted it as the closest thing the man had to a laugh.

"The Congo Desk has authorized me to use these diamonds to pay for weapons arriving from Kinshasa. The problem, Mr. Cushman, is that I don't know the proper value. The arms dealers will arrive with their experts. The Ugandans have deprived me of the locals. How do they say it in Texas? I need a ringer."

"In return for my services, you must agree to release Mr. Carpenter and promise my companions and I safe passage out of Kisangani."

"Most dealers work on a simple percentage basis," noted the general.

"I don't want your money."

"You are in no position to negotiate," General Kegama returned coldly. "Your life may not be worth much, but you seem to value your friends. If you don't do your job, I will execute your driver and Mr. Carpenter. I will turn this lovely creature into a barracks whore. She will be used a hundred times a day. Do you get the picture?"

"Vividly," said Lonny.

"Good." General Kegama issued instructions to his aide, who ushered two armed sergeants into the room. The first sergeant carried a flour scale, a cracked solar calculator, and a magnifying glass from a grade school science kit. The second sergeant carried a heavy brass artillery shell.

"What's that?" said Lonny.

"Your work."

The sergeant poured the contents of the big brass casing onto a blue UN tarp covering one of the long tables. A hundred thousand rough diamonds spilled chaotically into view: octahedrons, degraded cubes, spheres, shards, serrated fragments.

The Congo was littered with diamonds. Their source was volcanic pipes called kimberlites that brought superheated carbon to the surface of the earth. Over hundreds of millions of years, the volcanoes and their crystal-bearing lava were washed away by the incessant rain. The diamonds settled out in elbows of dead rivers buried beneath the forest.

The African population, decimated by Arab slavers, European Colonialism, the megalomania of their own despots, and the blight of Acquired Immune Deficiency Syndrome, clawed desperately in the mud for the geological debris. They had no government, no mail, no health care, no education. They lived in eternal present without any awareness of a future. As Clint Eastwood sneered in *The Good, the Bad and the Ugly,* "There are those with guns and those that dig."

The diggers traveled by cockleshell, dugout, and barge to the nearest settlement, where agencies traded the stones for antibiotics, plastic basins, batteries, knives, or yards of cloth. The agents then voyaged to Kisangani to sell their goods at one of the *comptoirs,* wholesale diamond counters. The general had collected many weeks' harvest in one artillery shell. If the green diamonds were still in Kisangani, they were on the table.

"You have four hours." General Kegama turned to leave, then turned back. "If so much as one stone goes missing, I will kill you all."

In the utter silence that followed the general's exit, Lonny realized that he had actually completed the first part of his mission. He had saved Alice's father from a well-deserved machete.

"I don't think I can do it," Lonny confessed to Tom Carpenter, while the two sergeants stood against the wall, watching their prisoners with malignant intensity.

"Why not?" demanded the deacon's father.

"The general will kill thousands of people if I help him."

"He'll kill us if you don't."

"I know. But after our journey here, I don't think I can contribute any further to the chain of death."

"Who gives a shit about these jungle monkeys?" Tom Carpenter lost his temper. "You made it here. Now you need to save my life!"

"Dad!" Alice stepped away from her father, whose hand she had been grasping for the last ten minutes. "Stop it!"

"You haven't seen the way these people act with each other. They hack each other over a cigarette. They prostitute themselves for a sip of beer. These aren't people like you and me, honey. They have AIDS."

"I can't believe you're capable of such filthy thoughts." Alice squinted at her father with both her eyes.

"I lost everything to these animals," said Tom Carpenter. "You have no idea, sweetie. I'm the real victim here."

"You're the victim? Look at us! I haven't changed my clothes in five days! I spent last night in the rain forest! Lonny and I nearly died trying to get here. Why didn't you warn us when we could still leave? In Kigali? Or Ruhengeri? Why did you trick us here? How could you be so selfish? Don't you care about anybody but yourself?" demanded Alice.

"There was absolutely nothing I could do to prevent your coming," Tom Carpenter excused himself. "I've been a hostage for six weeks."

"And the green diamonds?" Lonny decided to end the painful interview. "Where do you think they are?"

"You know about them?"

"Everybody from here to Hong Kong knows."

"They're in with all the others." Carpenter caressed the brass artillery shell. "I actually had them for a few hours."

"Did you buy them with the cathedral's money?" asked Lonny.

"A dealer offered them to me just before the general shut everyone down. It was too late to get out of the city."

"Then the stones belong to me," said Lonny.

"Are you trying to claim some of these diamonds?" demanded Alice.

"It's a technicality," Lonny replied.

"But you're not going to sort the stones, are you?"

"Of course I am." The image of his grandfather in Birkenau came to Lonny's mind, grading diamonds for a bowl of gruel and a stay of execution. If he wanted to see Annie again, he needed to do his job.

"Lawyers defend the guilty, priests hear confessions, diamantaires sort stones. That's what I do."

"Oh," said Alice, glancing from Lonny to her father. "You were just making a point."

"I think your father made his own points. But points are academic at the moment. If you want to live, you're going to learn how to sort rough. Let me show you how it's done."

Lonny plucked a stone from the pile and showed it to the Carpenters. "We're going to pick out all the diamonds that weigh more than a gram. Then we're going to weigh all the rest of this crap, which is called melee, into one-hundred-gram units." He held up the one-tenth of a kilo counterweight from the market scale. "We'll tie the melee into packets of cloth and salt a couple of large stones into each one. I'm going to set an average value of $500 a carat, per diamond, based on my knowledge of the trade. The shards are only worth $75 a carat, but the larger stones could be $5,000 or more. There are five carats in a gram. Each five-hundred-carat parcel will be worth $100,000."

"Is that what the general wanted?" asked Tom.

"It's the best we can do with the tools we've been given. We don't have time for anything else."

"I don't know if I can do it," said Alice.

"That's fine," replied Lonny. "In fact, it would be a great relief to me if you didn't touch a stone. Sorting diamonds is not a job for someone with a conscience."

Lonny tricked a sergeant into fetching Jean-Batiste by asking him to retrieve a case of soda and a cotton sheet from the back of the Toyota. The sergeant forced Jean-Batiste to carry the load through the terminal. As soon as the driver was inside the room, Lonny refused to let him leave.

They worked all morning with a cup of tea, some Cokes, and a few bananas for nourishment. Once the job began, the fascination of the stones diverted their attention from the purpose of their task.

Alice cut the bed sheet into squares. Tom and Jean-Batiste plucked out the largest stones while Lonny weighed and tied the diamonds into separate parcels. The armed sergeants scrutinized their every twitch.

Lonny came across the first green stone within an hour. A textbook example of a degraded carbon octahedron, two four-sided pyramids bonded at the base with concentric surface layers worn away by time. It was from an alluvial deposit millions of years old. The pick of the rain forest. The prize of the century.

He surreptitiously held the green diamond in the crook of his palm while he studied its shape and color.

Depending on the path of the light through the diamond, each one of the octahedron's icy planes presented Lonny with a subtle variation of green: mossy, absinthe, teal, sage, apple. When viewed at arm's length, the crystal appeared to be saturated an ethereal bottle green. His mind flitted through visual images of blue-yellow combinations until his memory's eye fixed on a hue from Germany, one that he had studied in a formerly beautiful city obliterated by American carpet-bombing during World War Two. Kurt Vonnegut's setting for *Slaughterhouse Five*—Dresden.

The Dresden Green was the cleanest green diamond in the world. In 1742, Frederick Augustus II, the King of Poland and regent of Saxony, purchased it for his capital city. He turned Dresden into a meeting place for music, philosophy, and literature. A special Green Vault was built around the 40.70 carat diamond in the royal palace. Its splendor outlasted two centuries of political maelstroms, Nazi propaganda, American bombers, and a forced visit to Moscow. The color of the diamond was so unique that aficionados, even the great philosopher Nietzsche, were at a loss to describe it by anything other than its own name, Dresden Green.

He found the other nine stones fairly quickly. He could glimpse their ethereal beauty along the edges of the lightly frosted skins. When these stones were polished, their final weight would range between one and three carats each. Holding them in his hand was a transcendent feeling of success. They were the color of his dreams. Congo Green.

He had traveled half the world through an unreported genocide and war. He had dodged a set of fakes and used his knowledge of language and custom to accomplish what no other gem dealer in the world dared. The achievement swelled his brooding heart with inordinate pride.

"We're even," Lonny said to Tom Carpenter, flashing him the stones.

The general came back when the sun was directly overhead, the heat intolerable, the act of breathing a labor.

"Are you finished?"

"Yes." Lonny showed him the two hundred and ten cloth bags. "The lowest measurement I could make was roughly $100,000 a bag. Some bags have more, some less."

"What's the total?" demanded the general.

"Twenty-one million dollars."

"It was worth the trouble to bring you here."

"And there are these." Lonny dropped eleven large diamonds into the general's hands. The ten Congo Green and one melon yellow. Lonny knew he would see them again.

"They're worth a million dollars each," he lied. As a suite they were priceless.

It took a moment for General Kegama to comprehend what he heard. "My Ugandan brothers are true bastards. It's no wonder they won't go back to Kampala!" He dropped the stones into his shirt pocket and buttoned the flap. "Sons of hyena bitches."

"Okay, okay," spat Viktor. He spoke with a heavy Eastern European accent. He was bald and slight. He squinted behind his cheap sunglasses. He reminded Lonny of a mole thrust into the sunlight.

General Kegama and Lonny sat at one table with their backs to the terminal. The Rwandan Patriotic Army was arrayed in a shallow crescent around their position, covering them with machine guns, sniper rifles, and mortars.

Viktor and three Israeli diamantaires sat on the other side of the table. They had arrived in an aging DC-3 that looked like a discarded aluminum soda can. The diamantaires wore plastic visors with magnifying lenses that could be snapped down in front of their eyes. They each had a mirrored tray, stainless steel stone sieves, long-handled tweezers, and an electronic scale.

"I tell you price. You give diamonds. If diamonds okay, plane lands." Viktor sounded unsure of himself. He didn't know who Lonny was, and he had every right to be wary of the general.

"Go," said the general, who had no taste for theatrics. "I want the same stuff you sold to the Ugandans."

"$10,000 minimum."

"No bullshit. $100,000 minimum," replied the general.

"Okay," said Viktor. "Fast business."

Lonny pushed a cloth bag of diamonds to the general, who gave it to Viktor, who handed it off to the diamantaires. They glanced up at Lonny as they pawed through the package like a panel of felonious rabbis.

The head buyer was none other than Ari Levi, a distasteful diamantaire Lonny had seen across the trading room in Ramat Gan but had never met. He was big-boned with a full beard and a fashionable yarmulke. Ari's accent was a cross between Brooklyn, East London, and Tel Aviv. In Antwerp, it was said that he could grab you by the nuts, stab you in the kidneys, and pick your pocket while simultaneously filing an arbitration complaint. Below his right eye, he had a large, round scar where an unhappy miner had plunged a corkscrew into his cheek. He was known as Amazon Ari for his Brazilian connections.

Apparently unaware that Lonny had spent his junior year abroad as an exchange student in Haifa, Ari spoke to the others in Hebrew.

"Watch me rip the bacon-eating grin off the *goyim*'s face." He gave the package back to Viktor, muttering English obscenities. "Worth $50,000 top."

Viktor pushed the bag back across the table. "Fix it."

General Kegama turned to the New Yorker.

Lonny stared at Ari Levi as he opened the cloth square on the table. He sorted through the material until he found the king stones carefully salted into each package. Each stone was about two grams in weight.

He was used to dealing with larger crystals, $10,000 to $350,000 a carat. These splinters of the rain forest were the lowest, least glamorous part of the trade. The only cutters with cheap enough overhead and labor costs to polish the material worked in India. There was no question in his mind that these stones would be faceted in Surat or Mumbai within seventy-two hours of entering the diamond pipeline. They would be transformed into earrings and bangles for the world's growing middle class. Polished and sanitized, the various dealers and retail jewelers could profess total ignorance of the direct connection between their goods and the genocide beneath the unending rains.

"Give me your scale." Lonny spoke in English.

Ari pushed one across the flimsy plastic table with an uneasy chuckle.

Lonny rolled the diamonds in his soft hands, weighing each of the king stones separately, then together. "9.34 carats, 13.22 carats. 22.56 carats in total."

Viktor, General Kegama, the diamantaires, and the soldiers watched the duel of wits between the two men. It was a game like any other, but each player waged vastly different stakes. Lonny played for his life, for the lives of his companions, and for the chance to see his daughter again. Ari played for purse and reputation. The gathered men took an interest in the outcome, like owners at a horse track betting on their stallions.

"May I have your loupe?"

"Get your own."

Lonny shrugged. He held each diamond up to the sun, shading his right eye with his right hand, quickly manipulating the stone in his left until he found the path that light followed through the carbon matrix. The diamonds were covered with a frosted skin that made it difficult to see much of anything. He evaluated the position of the various geltz by watching for deflected glints of sunlight. As a punishment for indifferent schoolwork, his father made him sort and reclassify melee from the age of twelve. He had peered into tens of thousands of stones, and his father had challenged each classification. Lonny's judgments had evolved to the point where they were unshakable.

"I learned to shape diamonds by carving apples when I was six years old."

"Your father was rich," countered Ari. "I learned on potatoes."

"I began cleaving stones during school vacation."

"My father couldn't afford to send us all to school. I cleaved stones so my younger brothers could eat," said Ari.

"I began sawing when I was sixteen."

"You started late."

"I've bruted, cut, and faceted thousands of diamonds."

"I still do."

"I worked as a brillianteer before I started to go blind."

"My poor sister is doing that job as we speak," replied Ari. "God save her."

The dealer leaned back to take Lonny's measure. Viktor stared at Lonny with renewed interest. General Kegama coughed. The two other Israeli diamantaires pulled at their shirtsleeves.

Polished diamonds are graded by the 4 c's: color, clarity, carat weight, and cut. The color is rated from D (finest white, river, exceptional white), down the alphabet to M (an unpleasing toilet-bowl shade of yellowish-brown). Clarity is rated from IF (flawless under

10X magnification) down nine grades to I3 (an opaque, commercial-grade stone as murky as a plastic milk carton). Once a stone is graded, it is simply a matter of weighing the specimen, adding a premium for a well-polished stone, subtracting for a bad cut, then tallying up numbers. There was little to it beyond simple accounting, which is why every dealer's son or daughter thought they could be a diamantaire in these days when certified lab reports substituted for an experienced eye.

The real money, however, was in the rough. The highest profit, and the highest risk, is made before a stone is polished, when not even the most experienced lapidary can vouch for the final product. Long odds and huge profit margins are the norm. Because of the up-front money required and the enormous risks, there were only a few dozen independent dealers in the world capable of buying, processing, and selling tens of millions of dollars' worth of raw diamonds outside the centralized pipelines originating in Southern Africa, Russia, Australia, Brazil, or Canada. And they all knew each other.

"I'll lay it out for you." Lonny made his case to the spectators, drawing on his near-photographic memory of the monthly pricing sheets. "The first stone is I color, eye clean. That makes it a VVS2 grade in the worst case. If it polishes out to four carats, emerald cut, you can sell it for $7,550 a carat wholesale." Lonny punched in the numbers and showed them to a clearly unimpressed Ari. "A $30,200 rock."

"The second stone is a little yellower, J color, VS1 clarity, 9 carat yield, $8,100 a carat. That means," said Lonny, punching the calculator, "$72,900 wholesale."

"Who says I want this crapola?" asked Ari.

"Together the polished stones will be worth $102,900. The rest of the lot, about $30,000 dollars, is pure profit. You're getting a thirty percent premium for this particular lot."

Viktor gazed at the side of his diamantaire's face thoughtfully, obviously unaware of his partner's margins. The general looked impatient enough to shoot someone.

But Ari appeared absolutely nonplussed with Lonny's speedy mathematical exposition. "You got lab reports, certified weights, proof of origin certification?"

"What the fuck is going on?" demanded Viktor.

"You're being sodomized by these *tokus* lickers," Lonny told him directly.

Ari cursed as if Lonny were trying to sell bad cheese.

Viktor repeated himself, "What the fuck?"

Lonny asked, "Are these guys buyers or appraisers?"

"We are the end users," Ari said with heavy sarcasm.

"I'll make it easy for you, Viktor." Lonny tumbled the two king diamonds across the plastic table toward the arms dealer. He took a business card with his office address on West 47th Street from his credit-card case and slid it across the table. "I will write you a hundred-thousand-dollar check for every bag of stones rejected by these *schmucks*. If they don't want to do business, you shouldn't have brought them. I know a good deal when I see it."

"You trying to cut me out?" Ari Levi screamed.

"That parcel is worth more than $100,000." Lonny jabbed his index finger into the diamonds. In Yiddish, he added, *"Der kush grobbe schteine."* Kiss my stones.

"Meshumed," returned Ari. Apostate.

"Are we kosher already?" Lonny switched to Hebrew. "Everybody is waiting for your blessing."

With the stares of Viktor and General Kegama boring holes into him, Ari Levi suddenly put two and two together. He snatched the business card out of Viktor's hand. "Leonard Cushman? Son of Caleb, son of Yitzhak? The one they call Lucky Lonny?"

"That's me, Amazon Ari."

Ari Levi raised both hands in the air, appealing to the indifferent sky, "He should be choked!"

"From your mouth to God's ears," Lonny returned. "I'm sure he listens to such a constant Jew."

If Ari had a gun, Lonny would have had a hole in his forehead. A purple rage blotted the dealer's face. His hands trembled, a vein on his neck throbbed like a garden hose, his pupils dilated. When the Israeli leaned over the table, General Kegama unholstered his pistol.

"Did you sort the rough?" demanded Ari, fulminating with anger.

"Every. Single. One." Lonny enunciated.

"Nothing fancy?"

"Not in this lot."

Ari stalked away from the table, buried his head in a towel, and wiped his sweaty face. Lonny almost starting singing the Kaddish, just to let Ari know how close he was to a bullet of his own making, but the Israeli snapped out of his rage as if flipping a switch. Like any experienced diamantaire, Ari knew fortune changed in the spasm it takes for a flawless stone to splinter on the lapidary's wheel. He exclaimed in Hebrew, "You could define a Jew's whole life by what shouldn't happen to him!"

Then he returned to the table with the kind of grin an orthodox rabbi plasters across his face after he's been told the next train to Auschwitz will leave on schedule. To the general he said in Yiddish, "*A brohk tsu dir.*" A curse on you.

He offered his paw to Lonny, "*Mazal und brucha.*" Luck and blessings.

They shook hands.

"Wonderful," said Lonny. Once the ancient Yiddish words were spoken out loud, the exchange was considered legally binding among diamantaires. It was an unheard of honor to concede the entire transaction without double and triple checking the material. But the circumstances were certainly unique.

"Okay, okay. Apologize for dumb motherfuckers," remarked

Viktor, shaking his head in disbelief. He radioed the code to the first cargo plane.

The general coughed dryly.

A DC-3 descended from the clear blue sky. There were patches on the wings. The twin engines spit gobs of oil that fell to earth like black rain. The fuselage was dented and shot through with jagged holes. It was a miracle that the battered machine was capable of flight. It bounced to a landing on bald tires, and the cargo door had to be pried open with a crowbar.

There was further positioning over the quality of the weapons that Lonny did not participate in and could frankly care less about. It seemed like the ancient plane was filled with enough ammunition to fight the Battle of Stalingrad. Fifty sacks of diamonds disappeared with the pilot. Fifty more sacks changed hands upon the arrival of a second DC-3, in even worse shape. Another three flights finished the transactions.

"I have tank," said Viktor.

"What kind?"

"Sherman tank. Fifty years Ukrainian National Museum."

"I'll take it."

"What you have?"

The general reached into his shirt pocket and extracted the cantaloupe yellow diamond. Amazon Ari and the two other Israelis burst into protest. Lonny raised one eyebrow as if to say, "I'll buy it for twice that price," and they nodded vigorously to Viktor. Even if he was bargaining for arms, Lonny simply could not allow another diamantaire to get the best of him. He was addicted to winning at any cost. It was the most despicable part of his nature and he knew it.

While the general and Viktor were inspecting crates of small arms, Ari Levi finally said to Lonny, "How about a little *rakhmones?*"

Lonny asked incredulously, "You want pity from me?" He knew the destruction of African villages in the Congo meant as little to the Israeli diamantaire as the torching of Ukrainian shetyls meant to Himmler.

"I'll take whatever I can get."

Lonny swiped a palmful of sweat off his brow. Although he would have liked to shoot Ari in the leg and watch him bleed out, the calming effect of crystalline hatred organized his vengeance in a more rational manner. "There's a Senegalese guy named Ibrahim, son of Muhammed. He drinks gin tonics. You know him?"

Ari shrugged, as if to say maybe he did, maybe he didn't.

"He beat me to the green."

"Why would you give me this information?" Ari demanded suspiciously.

"If you find him before I do," Lonny led him on, "I want you to send me some business. My father . . ." He shrugged his shoulders and let Ari imagine Cal's disappointment when he returned home empty-handed. Everybody in the trade knew about the tension between Lonny and his father.

Ari smirked. "If you eat sweets, you go to the dentist. If you dance with a *shiske,* you cry at the maternity ward. When you drink with the *shwartz* . . ." He made a hand-washing motion, as if to say, "It would have been better if you were not born." He spit on Lonny's shoes.

"My mother was a *shiske,*" Lonny said coldly.

Ari threw up his hands. "*Meshugene gens, meshugene gribbenes!*" Crazy parents, crazy children.

The general danced with the officers at the conclusion of the deal. His soldiers broke into the mountain of small arms ammunition, grenades, mortars, RPGs, and machine guns as if a bachelor uncle had packed their Christmas stockings. They fired a few mortars into the Ugandan section of the city and posed for digital photographs with the biggest machine guns resting on their crotches.

. . .

Lonny rejoined his companions in the concrete sauna. Alice and her father were having a heart-to-heart in the corner, Alice's voice rising and falling with her temper. Her father was soothing and implacable.

Alice was saying, "I trusted you, Dad."

"Circumstances spiraled beyond my control," replied her father.

"Mom was right."

"What did she say?"

"You're a liar."

"Alice, honey, you can't believe that."

"You used me."

"Not on purpose."

"You shouldn't have asked me for the money."

"That's all square now, honey. I settled it with your boyfriend."

"He's not my boyfriend. I spent the night with him because I was alone and confused."

"Well, it's settled."

"What do you mean?"

"It's between me and him. Don't worry about it."

A dry wind swept the airport, and the ground rippled as a massive Soviet-built twelve-cargo Antanov thudded to a landing. If the mile-long runway hadn't been designed and built by the CIA for Cold War shenanigans, the largest plane ever built would have rolled into the jungle. The gigantic wings exceeded the span of Lonny's imagination.

Four jet engines rent the air as a Sherman tank clanked and whirred down a hydraulic ramp. The battle tank was a deadly relic of a forgotten time, like a battle sword that has lain entombed for a thousand years. It was armor Franklin Roosevelt shipped to Joseph Stalin in the hour of his greatest need against Adolf Hitler. The Israelis disappeared into the cavernous cargo bay. Without turning off its engines, the Antanov swung into preflight position and hurled itself into the sky.

Lonny sat with his shoulders against the outside of the terminal, his legs splayed in front of him.

Jean-Batiste said, "They will make me into a *genocidaire* when you leave."

The gem dealer was playing with ten tiny pebbles the size of the green diamonds, walking the stones over his knuckles then marching them back again. He was working hard at reminding himself that despair was a vanity, as deceptive as joy.

"I'm granting you safe passage," said the general, tossing down three American passports. He pointed to the last DC-3 warming its engines.

"I want my driver." Lonny pointed at Jean-Batiste.

"Don't worry. I'll put him to work." General Kegama dropped the bottle-green diamonds from his breast pocket into Lonny's cupped palm. "Until you call me and tell me you have settled my private account."

"I've done everything you asked."

A flash of anger blazed across the general's face. "You don't want to cross me."

"I haven't crossed you," returned Lonny. "I have protected your interests no matter how much they revolt me."

General Kegama's lip curled. "Shall I keep the little whore too?"

Lonny arched his back against the wall and regained his feet. His father told him about an incident in Birkenau that had haunted Grandpa Cushman. Itzack woke in the middle of the night to discover his cap was gone. He reached over and stole a different cap from the next bunk. At roll call the next morning a man from the far end of the bunkhouse was shot for appearing bareheaded. Grandpa Cushman never came to terms with it and Lonny finally understood why. Like his grandfather before him, he had betrayed people that he would never meet.

Lonny clenched the ten green diamonds in his left fist and the gravel in his right. The general had made him an active participant in the genocide. The profit of his competitive eye would be used to murder innocent refugees, infect virgins with AIDS, mortar civilians, and starve children. The killing belonged to him. He owned it. In the fraction of the second it took the gem dealer to lift one fist and not the other, he refused to participate any further.

"Go to hell." He shoved the pebbles into the general's breast pocket.

General Kegama recoiled stiffly at his touch.

"I beg your pardon, general," Tom Carpenter stepped out of the terminal. "May I have a word with you?"

The general's face was as inscrutable as smoked ivory.

Lonny's left eye fluttered uncontrollably.

"I can arrange your private account. I have buyers."

General Kegama marched inside the terminal without a word.

"You're making a mistake." Lonny threw Tom's passport after him.

"This is the opportunity of a lifetime!" Carpenter snatched up his passport.

"Daddy!" Alice reverted to her worst, most infantile self, clutching at her father's arm. He gave her an exasperated look before scurrying after the general.

"*C'est ta chance, cours!*" Lonny murmured in French to Jean-Batiste. Run! The last DC-3 on the runway was sputtering black clouds of smoke. Jean-Batiste pushed off the wall and trundled away from the terminal as fast as his thick legs could carry him.

"Now." Lonny tugged Alice's hand.

Alice shook her limp, black locks. "Why would he do this?"

"Maybe," said Lonny, glancing away from Alice toward the runway, where Jean-Batiste frantically beckoned the pilots, "he only loves himself."

"What?" She stared at him.

"He was disbarred in New Jersey for stealing your trust fund."

"You can't prove it!"

"I don't have to prove it right now." Lonny raised his voice. "My job is to bring you home."

"I don't want to leave him."

Lonny took Alice by the shoulders, yelling to be heard over the increasing whine of the engines. "Remember when you came into my room? You promised me that if you had the choice between life and death, you would choose life. This is the moment I was talking about. You promised me."

She clenched her fists rigidly. "I know you're right, but I can't leave him."

"Do you want me to stay here and die?" demanded Lonny. "Because that's what you're asking of me. My daughter will be eight years old in two days. I'll never see her again if I don't get on that plane. Do you want that on your conscience?"

"I can't move my feet."

"What?"

"Take my hand. Pull me."

Lonny put his arm around her waist and took one step toward the plane. She hesitated, as if she were afraid of heights and they were about to walk along a cliff's edge, but she managed to put one foot forward and the other followed from habit. The struggle was entirely internal.

Lonny felt the eyes of the battalion follow their slow walk across the suffocating runway. The closing lines of the Nicene Creed inexplicably filled his mind: "We look for the resurrection of the dead and the life of the world to come." Even as he waited for a Tutsi sniper to stick a copper-jacketed bullet in the small of his back, he knew he would rather die trying to save Alice than return home without her.

Every small step across the endless tarmac seemed insignificant and wasted. The murderous sun beat down on their heads like a pair of angry fists and time stood still. Yet somehow they covered the two hundred yards separating the terminal from the DC-3 without being called back.

Jean-Batiste jumped from the rear cargo door of the plane and helped Lonny boost Alice inside. Lonny then scrambled aboard directly and grabbed an AK-47 lying on the flight deck. Alice sat stone-faced on a wooden box, as if the accumulated events of the past week had suddenly caught up to her and smashed her in the chest. She unconsciously tore at her cheeks with her dirty nails.

The gem dealer grappled up the slanted tube to the front of the plane with the assault rifle. He opened the cockpit door only to be greeted by Viktor waving a loaded Uzi from the co-pilot's seat. The Ukrainian pilot looked over his shoulder.

"Get us out of here!" Lonny shouted.

"What rush?"

"The general is going to destroy your plane." Lonny spun a web of lies as fast as he could twist them out of his mouth. "He thinks I'm working for you. He thinks we cheated him."

"Why?"

"He's convinced I fixed the prices with your Israelis. Because we spoke Hebrew and Yiddish."

"Not true!"

"Explain that to Kegama." Lonny pointed the barrel out the window to the terminal, where the general was pushing Tom Carpenter into a jeep, and ordering a platoon into a pickup truck. In fifteen seconds their escape would be blocked.

Viktor shouted at the pilot, "Go! Idiot!"

The veteran pilot pushed the throttles forward. A thousand loose rivets danced in worn sockets. The engines revved to an ear-splitting howl, and the plane groaned like a sick hippopotamus.

Lonny stumbled back down the cargo bay. Jean-Batiste balanced dangerously out the side door with an RPG on his shoulder. A flash singed Lonny's eyebrows as the ex-sergeant fired at the jeep. The rocket smacked the pavement short, skipped over General Kegama's head, and blew the front wheel off the pickup truck. The vehicle exploded in a ball of fuel, flipping end over end, spewing bodies and rifles into the air like plastic soldiers shaken out of a tin box.

"Push!" Jean-Batiste shoved a heavy wooden crate out the door. Lonny and Viktor did the same, kicking cases of live mortars and grenades onto the runway to lighten their load.

The laden plane was moving at only 50 mph, still 30 mph shy of its lift-off speed, and was a juicy target. The general's position between the terminal and the plane seemed to be the only reason the snipers on the roof of the terminal didn't blast them to kingdom come.

The jeep raced up to the rear cargo door in the prop wash. Alice popped her head out to scream hysterically at her father. General Kegama leveled his pistol at her head. Tom Carpenter tackled the general around the waist. Jean-Batiste flung Alice away from the door so Lonny could take her place with an AK-47. General Kegama executed Tom Carpenter. The force of the point-blank shot blew Alice's father off the back of the jeep, leaving him sprawled on the tarmac like an unconnected puzzle of bones.

The stern of the DC-3 lifted free of the runway as the general's driver raced to catch the accelerating plane one more time.

General Kegama fired at Lonny, hitting the door frame. Lonny put the rifle to his shoulder and sighted it on the jeep's hood. The general fired again. Lonny raised the barrel to the general's chest, not twenty feet away. Kegama continued to loose rounds at the gem dealer, but the jeep, bucking and swaying in the prop wash, prevented him from getting a clean shot.

"I'm sorry," Lonny apologized to God. If he was destined for hell, Kegama was going with him. He unloaded the rifle into the general's chest. The jeep rolled violently; steam billowed; muzzle flashes erupted like sun bursts from the terminal; the plane banked sharply into the sky and they were gone.

"We escape!" shouted Viktor, congratulating the three companions like kids who have outsmarted the class bully. They put their shoulders against the cargo door and forced it shut.

"Thanks to you," Lonny replied.

"Most diamond peoples . . ." Viktor flapped his hand side to side like a single-engine Cessna. "You straight ahead. I like you."

The plane bounced sideways knocking them all off their feet. If Lonny studied the thermodynamics of lift until his face turned blue, nothing would explain the miracle of that flying coffin.

"Where are we going?"

"Kinshasa."

Lonny banged his fist against the bulkhead. Kinshasa was almost as bad as Kisangani. Five warlords had joined together under international pressure to form the "government" of the Democratic Republic of Congo. Each warlord lived in a separate chateau belonging to the former dictator. Their thugs roamed the streets extracting food, money, and sex from the terrified populace. If the Rwandans were on good terms with any one of the warlords, Lonny would be met at the airport by a gang of heavily armed hoodlums. If he avoided that fate, he could count on being strip-searched and robbed the following day.

"You no like?"

"I want to go to Brazzaville, on the other side of the river."

"How much you give?"

Lonny collected all the money from his trousers and turned the pockets inside out. "$7,800. Everything I have." He neglected to mention the $800 zipped into his belt.

"Good business. I like Brazza." Viktor plucked the cash out of Lonny's hand.

"You know people in Brazza?"

"I have connections." Viktor gave Jean-Batiste a wink as he fanned himself with the hundred-dollar bills.

"You know," said Lonny, unable to help himself, "my family comes from Odessa."

"Like Alexander Pushkin?" Viktor referred to the father of Russian literature, a St. Petersburg aristocrat with one African grandfather.

"More like Isaac Babel."

Viktor nodded. "Don't worry, I no drop you in river."

They cut due east across the rain forest, leaving the wide Congo River to the right. Lonny caught glimpses of its scaled belly glinting in the afternoon sun. Conrad's nightmare. A 2,300-mile highway into the soul of evil. Each generation squeezed profits out of the moving water a different way—ivory, slaves, religious converts, rubber, diamonds. The benefits of endless war, of massacres without video cameras.

The ride over the storied river was remarkable for its sameness. There was no trace of Stanley's stone-crushing trek, of King Leopold's private ravages, or Rwanda's invasion and its millions of victims added to the original horror of '94. The blood had been washed away, the burned bones sucked into the whirlpools of memory. The forest canopy guarded its flesh-eating secrets like a green shroud. A string of phosphorescent red tracers soared impotently out of the trees and fell back to earth.

Lonny sat beside Alice on a pine box of rocket-propelled grenades.

"I'm sorry," he shouted over the deafening plane.

Alice's eyes were rubbed pink, and scratches marred both cheeks. She had glimpsed the final outcome with her nose pressed to a greasy porthole. Her pale face was a mass of confusion.

"I thought I could save him," she shouted.

"You did." Lonny felt the lost tenderness of their night together catch his voice.

"What do you mean?"

"He was thinking of you at the end. You have to remember that." Lonny put his arm around her shoulder. Tom Carpenter was a lying, thieving, back-stabbing bastard, but he had died to save his daughter. It was true. He might have loved her carelessly, but he loved her.

Alice collapsed against her chaperone and sobbed uncontrollably.

Lonny wondered how many Africans would have been spared if he had had the courage to absorb a machete blade instead of sorting diamonds for the general. Was it different for anyone else? Didn't his grandfather grade rough stones for the Nazis, aware the diamonds had come from the burned cavities of poisoned Jews, knowing his coerced expertise would finance the extermination of his own people? Lonny acknowledged that he couldn't have stopped himself if he'd wanted to. The will to survive is as universal and destructive as death itself.

Three hours after leaving Kisangani, they flew over the dim, smoky city of Kinshasa, Democratic Republic of Congo, and on to Brazzaville, Republic of Congo. It took a mere five minutes by air to cross the great, blood-brown river. Lonny knew that the same crossing by dugout or ferry would have cost his life if Rwandan spies caught up with them. A red-banded sunset yielded to darkness.

The pilot bounced down the unevenly lit runway in Brazzaville like a rodeo clown riding a bull's horns. As soon as they taxied to the terminal, Viktor leapt out to share backslaps and handshakes with military officers he addressed by their first names. The affable arms dealer had just as many friends on one side of the river as on the other.

"My pal, Major Didier." Viktor introduced Lonny, Jean-Batiste, and Alice to a rotund army officer before rushing off. "He take care of you."

"There are a few protocols we must observe," Major Didier announced in French. He was a middle-aged bureaucrat with skinny arms and legs married to a thick apple-shaped paunch. A few gray hairs showed above his temples. He wore a sky-blue polyester bowling shirt, brown pants, and flip-flops.

Lonny extracted a smooth half-carat diamond from the space between gum and upper lip. It was an adolescent trick, a method he had perfected to gain spending money outside the control of his tight-fisted father. Every diamantaire knew how to filch stones, if only because so many carats had been stolen from them.

"This should cover the protocols."

Major Didier good-naturedly slapped Lonny's palm with a generous amount of force. "It's nice to deal with a man who understands Africa."

The major escorted the three companions to a tin hovel clinging to the end of the white-washed terminal. Hyper-paced Congolese music blasted from a tinny radio, "Soukous, soukous, soukous!" There was one table in the middle of the zinc-roofed shack, rough benches around the edges. A portrait of the Republic of Congo's strong man confirmed it was an official government building.

The major stamped Lonny's and Alice's passports with purple entry visas.

"What about this one?" He looked at Jean-Batiste. "Is he American too?"

"We need you to help us, *monsieur*," said Lonny. "Without your wise counsel we are sure to spend many days in misery. I beg your assistance."

The official paged through the two American passports in front of him. He stared at Jean-Batiste, who stared back. Major Didier wagged his finger unhappily, "It will require a lot of work to arrange the papers. A lot of money. *Les papiers sont de la merde.*" A passport required shitwork.

"Thank you, Monsieur Didier," said Lonny. He felt a wave of relief at the mention of money. "Your youngest child will eat chicken and chips."

"I have eight children," Major Didier returned with a toothy grin.

"You are blessed," said Lonny, matching the official's pleasure. He took off his left shoe and shook out a diamond the size of a kosher salt crystal.

He had been through Brazzaville before and knew the routine. Although there had been civil war on this side of the river, the former French colony possessed a predictable code of corruption. Roadblocks were manned by uniformed men with flashlights. Peugeots, Renaults, and Citroens roamed the streets. In contrast to the other side of the river, where the desire for real laws had never been expressed, Brazzaville had a sheen of stability, like the iridescent shimmer on a soap bubble.

The major licked the diamond. "Viktor is a close friend."

They walked around the front side of the airport, neither as fascistically clean as the one in Kigali nor as battle scarred as the one in Kisangani. It was bustling feverishly like a prosperous village. Each new arrival of passengers or refugees injected fresh energy into the twenty-four-hour carnival. The next plane out was an Air Cameroon flight to Brussels, departing at midnight.

"You must get aboard that plane," directed Major Didier.

The major herded them past phalanxes of policemen. It surprised Lonny to see himself in a mirror. He had been wearing the same suit for a week. His blue shirt was gray and stained with blotches of sweat, perhaps blood. His short hair had coagulated into patches, where it wasn't singed off. He had the makings of a beard. His pants were destroyed.

"Yikes!" Alice practically jumped away from her reflection. "I'll be right back."

Major Didier led Jean-Batiste toward a back office to begin rounds of ass-kissing and bribery.

The Air Cameroon ticket counter was jammed cheek-to-jowl with Africans at least twenty deep pleading their cases. Lonny circled the rear of the pack. He saw a woman in a blue airline uniform near the baggage claim.

"*Pardon*," said Lonny.

"What happened to you?" replied the clerk in French. Her long hair was twisted into hundreds of tiny braids and wrapped stylishly around the top of her head. She wore polished leather pumps and a little name tag.

"I am a refugee."

"Evidently."

"I'm also a diamond merchant."

"Oh?" She perked up a little.

"I have family in Belgium."

"You're Belge?"

"American. But I love Belgium." He enlarged the fib.

"What can I do for you?"

"I would like to buy three tickets to Brussels."

"We're sold out."

"Even first class?"

She crinkled her nose. "Follow me."

Alice reappeared as they were hurrying toward a closed ticket counter. She wore a baggy sundress tied tight to her body with a set of cotton wraps. The colorful cotton cloth was imprinted with a French idiom, "*Ne pleure pas comme une Madeleine.*" Don't Cry for Nothing. Her hair had been brushed out loosely.

"It's amazing what you can get for a pair of dirty blue jeans."

The clerk said to Lonny, "I'll need your credit card."

"Do you have seats?"

"Don't be stupid."

Lonny tactfully gave one of his charge cards to Alice who handed it to the clerk. The clerk shared that exasperated "Men are so impossible" eye-roll with her white American sister.

"I'll find Jean-Batiste." Lonny beat a strategic retreat.

Crackling tension filled the airport the closer the hour hand moved toward midnight. Policemen, immigration officials, customs officers, baggage screeners, army personnel, petty bureaucrats, and functionaries all had to extract their wages out of the departing passengers. Fat businessmen quietly passed folded notes to their tormentors. African women were forced to undo their bundles again and again until they placated merciless boys younger than their own sons. There were only a dozen Europeans, Lebanese, or Greek businessmen. The officials fought over them as if they were ATM machines in need of the right PIN code.

"Look at me!" Jean-Batiste grabbed Lonny's arm. He held up a shiny red passport with his picture: Jean Congo from Brazzaville. Major Didier had disappeared.

"You changed your name?"

"I must have a new name to be a new man."

"What about your family name?"

"It was a fiction from the day I was born. I refuse to be a Hutu or a Tutsi."

"What are you then?"

"A New Yorker."

"You can drive a cab if you learn the boroughs and the bridges."

"Can I live with you?"

"Of course." Lonny grasped the Rwandan's hand, picturing Jean-Batiste as the superintendent of his townhouse. "We'll park your taxi right out front. My neighbors will turn green with jealousy!"

Jean-Batiste hugged Lonny. Not the customary Rwandan embrace, which guards a certain hygienic distance, but a full bone-crushing clench. "New York will love me!"

The gem dealer ushered Jean-Batiste to the airline counter where he gave their three passports to the Air Cameroon representative.

"*Bravo*," the woman applauded Jean-Batiste's document.

The distance between the ticket counter and the airplane was measured in the number of people left to bribe. Lonny hoped the eight hundred dollars left in his money belt would get them all aboard.

The policeman manning the metal detector told Lonny to empty his pockets. The machine was useless at picking up diamonds, but not to seem suspicious, he took off his shoes and put them on the conveyor belt. Alice had nothing except her passport. Jean-Batiste carried the keys to his red Mercedes.

Immigration was next, where all three travelers discovered Major Didier had not stamped exit visas into their passports. It cost Lonny five hundred dollars from his money belt to clear up that misunderstanding. He was down to his last three hundred dollars in cash.

The Ministry of Finance came after immigration. They demanded to count all of Lonny's money. They took two-thirds when they found out that he didn't have a Foreign Currency Declaration stamped by themselves.

Lonny headed into the final security screening with a hundred dollars left. When he realized that he would be patted down in a zippered vinyl booth occupied by a customs officer, he stepped out of line for the bathroom.

Inside the smelly water closet he removed all ten green diamonds from the elastic waistband of his boxer shorts. The rectum is a small chamber at the end of the small intestine about three inches long. With a finger it is possible to insert a case the size and width of a large thumb past the rectum onto a kind of shelf in the small intestine. Some diamantaires tried it once in their entire lives; others used the body cavity on a regular basis. Lonny gritted his teeth and poked the diamonds past his sphincter, one by one.

Inside the booth, the customs officer refused to look him in the eye. He fingered the seams of his pants, in case it held a sword, checked the elastic of his boxers for detonators, and the inside of his belt for any spare bills. The officer never said a word and neither did the gem dealer, but Lonny couldn't help but notice that his last hundred-dollar bill disappeared. He looked hard at the officer. The skinny man dared him to say something that would give him all the permission he needed to club the living daylights out of the foreigner.

"Have a nice night." Lonny put one foot in front of the other and nobody killed him. Climbing aboard the air-conditioned jet liner was like crossing a portal to a different universe. The clean rug, the plastic overhead bins, the bright lights. A stewardess showed him a wide, first-class seat beside Alice. Jean-Batiste sat across the aisle in a window seat. The stewardess offered him a damp towel and a glass of orange juice. The physical contrast between the two worlds, side by side, existing within one another, couldn't have been more startling than if Lonny had seen a live jinni stare at him from the end of a cigar.

He peeked behind the curtain into the tourist section. The majority of the seats were empty.

"How much did I pay for these three seats?"

"$15,984," said Alice, showing him the receipt. "One way."

The diamonds grated uncomfortably inside his rectum. "I need to use the bathroom."

"*Attend trois minutes, monsieur,*" intoned a fashionable stewardess. Wait, three minutes. The soldiers beyond the window had no effect on her. A car sped up to the staircase and a last passenger tramped up the stairs, one who had obviously not suffered through the indignities of multiple security screenings. The President's son or a minister. Lonny closed his eyelids.

"*Leonard?*" A voice boomed down the cabin.

Lonny opened his eyes to the sight of the huge Senegalese diamond merchant squeezing sideways down the aisle.

"You're alive!" Lonny rose to shake Ibrahim's hand.

"No thanks to you."

"I gave you a head start."

"You did." Ibrahim sat across the aisle from Lonny, next to Jean-Batiste, overruling the stewardess's objections as the door closed.

"I made the transaction," Ibrahim said triumphantly.

"When?"

"An hour ago on the other side of the river."

"Who?"

"Israelis. Very rude people."

"Did one of them have a round scar on his cheek?"

"Yes," returned Ibrahim. "You know him?"

Lonny squeezed his hands together in delight at the idea of Amazon Ari buying a fake suite of green diamonds. The financial loss would cause him more pain than a case of shingles. "Let's just say, you should forget about visiting Tel Aviv any time soon."

"Nine million," Ibrahim bragged.

Lonny punched the dealer on the arm. "Not bad!"

Ibrahim replied seriously, "It's impossible to know if they were enhanced."

"You'll marry a princess," commented Lonny with genuine pleasure.

"I will pick the prettiest daughter. I will travel to Mecca. She will bear me seven children."

"And my commission?" Lonny reminded the Senegalese of their last-minute arrangement. Ten percent of the sales price after costs.

"Leave it with me. I will invest it for you in Senegal, and one day you will visit your riches like a forgotten son."

"*Mazel en broches,*" said Lonny. Luck and blessings.

The stewardess arrived with the chief pilot in tow. He wore more gold braid than an emperor. "I will not fly the airplane until you are in your proper seat."

"I'd move if I were you," commented Lonny. "You don't want to pay full price."

"*Shalom,*" said Ibrahim. Peace.

"*Salaam alekam,*" Lonny replied. Peace be with you.

The Senegalese dealer moved past the curtain to the tourist section, where Lonny heard him loudly rearranging the passengers for his own convenience.

"We did it," Lonny said to himself, as the jet accelerated toward thousands of miles of impenetrable jungle, countries aflame with ethnic strife, the Sahara, and the Mediterranean Sea.

"*Ehh-ben!*" cried Jean-Batiste when the wheels left the ground. "I hope the people in America behave better than the ones in Africa."

Lonny translated the sentiment for Alice. She leaned across the gem dealer and spoke to the driver. "Don't be so damn naïve."

"Ms. Carpenter," Lonny chuckled. "The seminary is not going to know what to do with you!"

9 Annie's Birthday

The year Lonny turned eight was the worst of his life. His mother committed suicide by stepping out a seventeenth-story window. She bounced off the sidewalk as he skipped home from PS 218 for his afternoon *gouté*. His father couldn't bear to look at him, so he was packed off to boarding schools in Connecticut for the next ten years. In one stroke he lost both his mother and his father, and he had been emotionally orphaned ever since.

He refused to let the same thing happen to Annie. As soon as the Air Cameroon plane landed in Brussels on Monday morning, exactly seven days after he had left it, he hustled Jean-Batiste and Alice onto an Aer Lingus flight to John F. Kennedy Airport. A quick check of his messages revealed that Cass was taking Annie and three friends to see *The Lion King* at 8 p.m. that night. He absolutely had to be there for her eighth birthday party.

The companions were severely delayed extracting Jean-Batiste from the clutches of the U.S. Immigration and Naturalization Service. The immigration officers, as callous as the ones in Africa, regarded the red Congolese passport with undisguised racism. They fingerprinted the driver and were about to send him to a holding cell on Rikers Island when Alice got through to a pro bono lawyer at the Immigrant's Resource Center. It wasn't until 5 p.m. that the INS agreed that Jean-Batiste's claim of political asylum could be reviewed before a judge in six months.

As they departed the grimy, crumbling airport, Jean-Batiste used his impeccable French to grill the Haitian taxi driver threading potholes on the Van Wyck Expressway.

"You like the work?"

"I think about today not the past."

"Have you ever seen Rwandans around here?"

"What's a Rwandan?"

Jean-Batiste sat back in the cab and said to the skyline, "I'll show these Haitians."

"Grenades won't help." Lonny gestured to the five lanes of traffic merging toward Manhattan.

They pulled up to the curb in front of the gem dealer's half-renovated townhouse on East 64th Street. Monday afternoon, 6 p.m., and the construction crew clearly had not been there for the past week. Lonny installed Jean-Batiste in a fourth-floor suite. It had a bay window with clear view of the street and a rear exit for emergencies. He was going to sleep easier with the imperturbable Kigali native staying under the same roof.

"I'm just beginning to understand what you've gone through," Alice said to the driver.

Jean-Batiste embraced her, replying in French. "You're the first student priest I ever hugged. America!"

Lonny accompanied Alice back to the Cathedral of St. John the Divine. The rusted scaffolding reminded him simultaneously of the cranes in Kisangani and Poe's House of Usher. The Episcopal church had already seen its future come and go. There wouldn't be any more Episcopal presidents like Franklin Delano Roosevelt to quarry stone with government funds. A crack had appeared in the foundation of the church, invisible to those who worked inside, but glaring to the casual worshipper. Deacon Carpenter and the Bishop of Rwanda co-existed as uneasily within the same moral architecture as Congolese blood and high fashion.

They stood in the cathedral garden near the statue of the enormous, diabolical crab dangling innocent creatures from its pincers.

"I was wrong to take your money and give it to my father."

"He and I settled that debt in our own way," replied Lonny. "It's not your concern anymore."

"Are we still friends?"

Lonny glanced at his watch. "I don't think you're going to need a chaperone again any time soon."

She laughed nervously. "I think you're the most honest person I ever slept with, and you're not that honest."

Dean Addison came striding down the walk. If the church were organized along corporate lines, his title would have been senior vice president. He was in charge of the cathedral, more powerful than a parish priest, less important than a bishop. His wife was also an Episcopal priest. She had once shown Lonny her "diamond" engagement ring, a superbly polished cubic zirconium.

"Well, look who's here. Our youngest deacon and the newest member of the board of trustees. I'm so glad you're back safely."

Alice shoved the dean, almost flattening him. "Liar."

Lonny pulled the dean back to his feet. "Tom Carpenter was executed before our eyes in the Congo."

"Dear God." Dean Addison regarded his most junior deacon warily.

"He was facilitating the exchange of diamonds for weapons."

"How awful."

"He got the money from you, Dean. My money."

"Yes." The dean bowed his head as if he had nothing to do with it. "A terrible business."

"I want you to replace that money yourself," said Lonny.

"St. John's is bigger than either of us, Mr. Cushman."

"That's why I need to make sure you do the right thing." He

gripped the dean's limp hand, holding him close. "I want you to take full responsibility for your actions. Don't even think about laying it off on Ms. Carpenter."

The dean drew himself up to his full height. "I hoped to protect this institution from one bad decision on my part. I thought you might also agree to protect our good name if you understood the pressures of administration and fund-raising."

"Liar!" Alice exploded. "You took advantage of me! You knew my father was going to Rwanda for blood diamonds. And now you want the moral high ground?" She pulled back her fist.

"Control yourself!" The dean dodged behind Lonny.

"You're a coward." Alice menaced him again just to watch him flinch.

"You have thirty days." Lonny extricated himself from the dean's grasp. "I will bring criminal charges against you and sue for damages in civil court if you don't replace the money. I assume your signature was on the back of my check when it cleared the bank."

"Think of the church!" cried Dean Addison in dismay.

"I am thinking of the church."

Alice stared at the dean with a cold fury that surprised even Lonny. "You'll probably wiggle out of this, but I'm going to make sure your wife knows who you are before it's over."

"My wife has nothing to do with this."

"She deserves to hear what we were doing Friday afternoons on my futon."

"You've gone too far!" Dean Addison shook his head like a disapproving confessor.

"There she is now," said Alice, waving energetically to a figure on the far side of the tangled garden. "Snake man."

The dean backed slowly away from Alice, then ran toward the church offices as if they would offer him some protection against the coming storm.

"You've traveled a very long way." Lonny kissed her on the cheek.

"I'm sure you'll make a terrific priest."

Alice kissed him on the other cheek. "Thank you for bringing me home."

Lonny set out on Amsterdam Avenue at 112th Street, turning on Broadway and following it uptown toward 42nd Street. It was 7 p.m.; cabs blew by without stopping. He struggled with the connection between how he had survived and how he wished to live: Kisangani and West 47th, the demolished African embassies and the scalloped skyscrapers, his divorce from Cass and his future with Annie.

His intimacy with the dead, the dying, and the soon-to-be-butchered sharpened his awareness of the familiar cityscape. Mirrored limousine windows reflected women's legs sheathed in nylon and striding forward on sculpted heels, as scentless as glass flowers. But a tall pile of rotting garbage brought back visions of all the decaying cadavers beside checkpoints in Central Africa. Their silence filled his bones. Their lifeless orbs stared at him from the sockets of strangers.

Annie squealed with delight at the presence of her gaunt father in the lobby of the Broadway theater. Lonny made the evening show of *The Lion King* just in time for the 9 p.m. break. Beefy American actors were dressed up as East African plains animals, singing songs to an urban Soweto beat. The young lion was a Californian with fabulous pectorals. Most of the audience were children who had already seen the production as a feature-length cartoon.

"Daddy!"

Lonny lifted her off the carpeting. She pressed her cheek against his.

"I knew you'd come back from Africa."

"How'd you know that?" Lonny spied Cass approaching him across the lobby.

"You promised me!"

"Happy birthday! My big eight-year-old!"

"There aren't any gorillas in the play, but there is a monkey!"

"Lucky gorillas."

"Can I have twenty dollars? I'm with Caitlyn, Selma, and Hadley."

Cass poked Annie on the shoulder. "Nice try. We're going out after the show."

"Please, Dad."

"Listen to your mother."

Annie petulantly threw back her head. "Put me down."

"I'll always be here for you," said Lonny. Tears brimmed on his lower eyelids before he was able to vanquish the emotion.

Cass was as beautiful as ever in that Upper East Side way. Streaked blond hair, cornflower blue eyes, healthy skin bathed, massaged, and perfumed. Her Dolce & Gabbana halter top and embroidered white jeans completed the effect.

"I found out how much you're worth."

"So what?" replied Lonny. "You sleep with people who make me look like the doorman."

"I want my share."

"Excuse me?"

"You were in the Congo buying blood diamonds."

"There are no such things as blood diamonds. Just diamonds and people who use them for their own purposes."

"Tell it to the law guardian."

Lonny stared opened-mouthed at his ex-wife. He wanted to say, "I've seen women's bodies stacked like mangoes." He wanted to say, "It's not all about you." He wanted to say, "Do you know who I had to kill to get here tonight?" And then, as he saw his father elbowing through the intermission chatter with grim determination, he felt utterly exhausted. The theater's golden plaster and tasseled curtains emphasized the true emptiness of his family life.

"How much do you want?"

"Twenty million dollars."

"Why?"

Cass shook out her hair. "I need my independence."

"This isn't about Annie?"

"Not really."

"You'll agree to joint custody?"

"Absolutely."

"One week at your place, one week at mine?"

"Yes."

"Switch on Mondays?"

"Sure."

"Alternate vacations. You get Thanksgiving, I get Christmas."

"You've thought about this." Cass appeared temporarily at a loss.

"I want a real relationship with my child, not just two weekends a month."

Cass planted a soft kiss on the side of his mouth, a strange reminder of the nights she used to greet him at the door of her apartment in a low-cut blouse, thigh-highs, and heels. "Annie loves you more than any other man in the world." She frowned sourly at the approach of her ex-father-in-law. "Call my lawyer when you've got the dough."

Cal thumped his son on the back. "He lives." To Cass he said, "Great show."

Cass nodded vacantly. "If you'll excuse me . . . the third act is about to begin." She batted both eyes at Lonny then brusquely stepped between two tourists from Iowa marveling over the price of a T-shirt that said, "I saw The Lion King on Broadway."

In response to his father, Lonny said, "It was close, that's for sure."

"I told you not to go."

"Isn't it boring to be right all the time?"

Cal shook his graying head. "Not at my age. Come grab a coffee."

They pushed out of the theater toward Times Square. The neon signs and plasma screens glittered brilliantly in the cool night hours. The crawl beneath a newscast read, "Rwanda blocks war crimes investigations in the Congo, accuses UN Peacekeepers of child rape . . ." In this supposedly interconnected and global world, it was hard to comprehend that New York City and Kisangani existed on the same planet.

Cal bought two cups of coffee and directed Lonny to the back of the New Amsterdam Deli. They sat by themselves at a small metal table.

"I had to kill a man," Lonny admitted. "Two actually."

"It doesn't show." Cal ignored his son's complaints.

Lonny examined his hands thoughtfully. "Is that all you have to say?"

"There's a pair of pigeon-blood rubies for sale. I think we should buy them."

"How much?"

"It's not the price that matters," pitched Cal. "It's the color and the provenance. Clear pigeon blood. The stones were presented to the King of Afghanistan by the Shah of Iran."

"You've seen the stones?"

"Extraordinary."

"What are they asking?"

"Three million for the pair."

"Why hesitate?"

"I want my junior partner's opinion."

Lonny reached into his shirt pocket and pulled out the price-less suite of green diamonds. He laid them before his father. "We're equal partners."

Some people become coarse and excitable when they are nervous. Cal Cushman was the opposite. The more unsettled he became, the calmer he behaved. He glanced at the green diamonds on the table-top as if they were cheap emeralds. He casually pulled out a loupe, fixed it in his eye, then moved the stones into focus. He placed a pocket scale on the table.

"Nine stones, 22.871 carats." He switched on a pocket xenon

flashlight and laid the colored diamonds on the lens.

"What do you mean nine stones?"

His father funneled the stones through a paper place mat onto the formica table. "One, two, three, four, five, six, seven, eight, nine. I count nine."

Lonny rifled through three inside suit pockets, his two outside suit pockets, the breast pocket, the watch pocket, his two rear pants pockets, his front right pocket, his front left pocket, the coin pocket. He couldn't imagine what had he done with the tenth diamond.

"Check your shirt pocket," said Cal. "Either it's there or it's not."

"You do it."

Cal patted the outside of the pressed shirt. "Could be."

Lonny reached cautiously into the shirt pocket and plucked out the largest stone. "That was close."

"Ten stones," recapped Cal, weighing them together. "29.134 carats. What color would you say?"

"Congo Green."

Cal bit his cheek. "What's the provenance?"

"I took them off General Kegama. A Tutsi *genocidaire*."

"You think they've been zapped?"

"Absolutely not."

"Would you stake your reputation on it?"

"They are the finest suite of natural green diamonds ever brought to market."

Cal folded the green diamonds separately into ten crisp diamond papers. "We'll see what the gem lab has to say. If they've been super-cooled, radiated, and annealed, they'll show a spectrum absorption line at 595 nanometers."

"Why can't you take my word for it?"

"Why should I?"

"My feel for colored diamonds is as good as yours."

Cal smirked. "I'd rather not revisit your teenage angst."

"I've put our firm on the map for another generation." Lonny leaned across the deli table. "You can afford to acknowledge it."

"How about the truth?" Cal rapped his knuckles on the table.

"I'd welcome it."

"It's about time you pulled your weight." The older man massaged his wrinkled forehead with his age-spotted hands. "You've cost me more grief than a bankruptcy."

"That's the best you can do?"

"What more do you want from me?"

Lonny left his coffee cup on the table and bought his first pack of cigarettes in years. He fired up outside the deli while Cal hailed a cab. Ads for business products and the action movies lit the night. Packs of drunken twenty-year-olds crashed into slow-moving rubberneckers. Two of New York's finest surveyed the scene with amused detachment.

He broke the filter off the end of his nicotine stick and sucked the bitter smoke deep into his lungs. The ashen taste in his mouth brought to mind the Rwandan church filled with ghosts. He realized why they hovered in limbo between this world and the next. They refused to accept the killing perpetrated in their name. Forgiveness was the eternal prayer of the innocent and the guilty, the discarded and the powerful, the dark forest and Times Square, his mother and himself, Alice and her father. Acceptance was the only solution.

Lonny stepped on his cigarette the instant he saw Annie and her friends leaving the theater. He rushed across 42nd Street. Her radiant joy reminded him of what it was like to be eight years old and filled with grace.

Cass herded the children down the bright sidewalk. Lonny snuck up behind them, grabbed Annie's hand, and sprinted ahead, dodging pickpockets, shills, and undercover detectives. They ducked into the foyer of a building to hide from the pursuing posse. His eyes leaked hot, saline rivers when he caught a whiff of his daughter's bubblegum-scented hair. She giggled as her friends ran by.